Family Smarts

&

Runaway Hearts

KC Hart

A humble gift to my heavenly Father who is always there to bring me back when I run away.

Books By KC Hart

A Christmas Blaze

Fresh Starts and Small Town Hearts

Business Smarts and Reckless Hearts

Car Smarts and Bashful Hearts

People Smarts and Wounded Hearts

Kid Smarts and Wistful Hearts

Family Smarts and Runaway Hearts

Elsie: Prairie Roses Collection

Moonlight, Murder and Small Town Secrets

Music, Murder and Small Town Romance

Memories, Murder and Small Town Money

Merry Murder and Small Town Santas

Medicine Murder and Small Town Scandal

Marriage, Murder & Small Town Schemes

Mistaken Murder & Small Town Status

Mistletoe, Murder & Small Town Scoundrels

Join KC's newsletter and receive a free ebook of Music Smarts and Humble Hearts

Chapter One

"Red said you're leaving at the end of the week." Floyd stepped up to the food truck window where Quinn Lewis waited for his sausage dog. The roar of the cement mixer several yards away hummed out of sync with an old George Jones tune blaring from somebody's truck. "I'm supposed to talk you into staying until the hotel is finished." He glanced over his shoulder at the new three-story building that would soon be Red Creek, Alabama's first luxury hotel. "We'll be done in another month or so. What's your rush?"

Quinn Lewis took his sausage dog from the burly bald man in the off-white t-shirt with stained armpits and orange BBQ sauce splattered across his sizable chest. "Thanks, Eric." Tattoos covered every part of the food truck owner's body, from his chest to his wrists, but the big guy sure knew how to make a sausage dog. Quinn paid for his lunch, then turned to Floyd. "We've been cramped up in that little travel trailer together for six months. Nothing personal, but I'm pretty sick of you." He pulled the wax paper away from the soft steamy bun and took a bite of his meal. He glanced back at the food truck where the young woman in the hairnet and baggy sweatshirt worked behind Eric. She kept her head down as she pulled the sausages from the warmer and put them in the steamed buns, then wrapped them in the flimsy papers. "It's time to get back to God's country."

"Awe, man." Floyd spat a brown puddle of tobacco juice into the dust near Quinn's mud-crusted steel toed work boots. "You're always out with a girl when we're not working. We barely see each other, much less get on each other's nerves." He wiped the back of his hand across his mouth. "Think about all the money you are going to be leaving on the table if you go now."

"I can't help it." Quinn looked down at the man he had shared the tiny lodgings with ever since coming to town to work the construction job. "I miss my momma and the rest of my family. I've got to go."

"I sure do hate it." Floyd trailed along beside Quinn over to one of the rackety picnic tables where men were sitting eating their lunch. "I'll have to pay your half of the rent until I can find somebody to take your spot. My wife won't like it. She's depending on the money I send to her."

"Sorry, man." Quinn threw one of his long legs over the wooden bench and straddled the seat. Floyd could spin a pitiful tale, but he wasn't fooling Quinn. He would have a new renter lined up for Quinn's end of the travel trailer before he drove off the lot on Friday.

Quinn watched Floyd walk away. He didn't have anything against the man or the job or the town or even the state of Alabama. They were all fine, but they weren't Carson's Bayou. When he'd gotten laid off from the oil field last fall, he'd been thankful Langston Wade had told him about this job and helped him get on with its crew. He was not in dire straits when it came to money, quite the opposite. He'd been investing most of his earnings for the past decade and could have easily made it for a long, long time on his nest egg money. When he was still out of work through Thanksgiving and then Christmas; however, he knew he had to go to work or go stir crazy.

Now it was time to go home. He took a drink from his Gatorade bottle. The constant whirring of the cement mixer, the muffled chatter of different conversations, the music from the overzealous country music fan who shared his tunes from his enormous truck speakers with everyone there, gave the work site an almost festive vibe. It wasn't a bad job, and it definitely wasn't any harder than the offshore job he had before, but the truth of the matter was, Quinn was lonely. Sure, he went out on the weekends with some of the guys and usually had a date from the little town, but these people didn't know him, the real Quinn Lewis. The only people that truly knew him were his brothers, Drake and Hank. Even his momma didn't know him as well as she thought she did.

He shoved the last bite of the sausage dog into his mouth and wadded up the flimsy wax paper. A whistle blew across the yard, and he stood up. Time to get back to work. He tossed his empty drink bottle and the paper in the trash barrel and strode across the dusty ground toward the building that would soon be completed. He reached into his shirt pocket and pulled out a sour apple jolly rancher and unwrapped it. Sensing eyes upon him, he turned and looked toward the food truck. The woman who had fixed his food met his eye. He smiled, and she looked away.

Was she Eric's wife or his sister? She was always there working and always silent. She seemed lonely too, or was he just pushing his feeling off onto her? She was the only female on the site. What would make a woman choose that type of job? Tomorrow he'd speak to her, thank her for cooking his food. She probably didn't hear that often. These men were good enough folks, but most of them were a little rough around the edges. Not all of them. There were a few Bible thumpers like his brother Drake. One of them may have thanked her for working the long days in the hot little truck for probably very little pay, but maybe they hadn't. It didn't matter either way. She looked like a sad little gnome in her black hair net and baggy clothes. He could brighten her day before he left. He popped the piece of candy in his mouth, continued across the yard, and headed back to work. Two more days, then he could get back home. Maybe then this longing for—something— would ease.

Ollie rolled the sausages over on the griddle, her mind wandering to other things. The steamy aroma of frying pork rose with the sizzle of the meat, unnoticed as it saturated her hair and clothing again today. Would she ever smell like some-thing other than sausage? Dad said his stomach growled every time she walked in the room. She shifted her feet in the cramped workspace, careful not to bump into Eric standing in the window area as he passed out the food and collected the money.

When she had first fallen from grace and started working for the man, he had put her in the window serving the construction workers their food. That had lasted an entire thirty minutes before Eric demoted her to sausage flipper. When she had handed a worker, who seemed to see himself as a Don Juan of the south, his lunch, he made a disgusting remark about sausages. She reacted without thinking—her fist in his face. That was the story of her life, though, acting first and thinking later. Now she was working in a food truck, and not just in a food truck, in the back of a food truck where she couldn't screw things up.

At least Eric hadn't fired her that day. The louse with the bloody nose had gotten a free lunch, and a warning from Eric that if he harassed her again, the next punch would be from him which would land the guy in the hospital. Eric could do it, too, no doubt.

"Ollie, look, let's remove temptation and let you flip for a few days," Eric had said, "until the men get used to a woman being in their midst."

"Temptation?" Ollie snorted, looking down at her grease stained t-shirt. "I'm sweating like a pig and this hair net is not exactly a fashion statement, Eric. That man was just being a jerk."

"You're probably right, but let's move you to the back. Most of these men are working away from their wives and girlfriends, and a lot of them don't know how to act around a lady, anyway." He wiped his enormous hands on the dish towel tucked in his jeans. "I can't have you punching every guy in the face who comes on to you, or the foreman will have me run off the site."

"Come on to me?" Ollie wiped the back of her hand across her forehead. "He was being a horse's patoot."

"That's the way idiots flirt, Ollie." The bear of a man grinned. "Here." He handed her a pair of tongs. "You flip for a while. I'll run the window. Just to be safe."

She had been the flipper ever since. It was for the best. Her thoughts pulled back from her musings as the conversation at the window caught her attention. Quinn Lewis was leaving town? She dropped the sausage in the bun and took a step closer to where the men chatted as she wrapped the meat and bread in wax paper. She had been listening to all the workers every day, trying to pick out the best one to work her scheme on. So far, she had three candidates: Quinn Lewis,

Donny West, and Andrew Norman. If Quinn Lewis was leaving town on Friday, that put him as the top contender.

The tall man with the scruffy beard and shaggy hair pulled back in a ponytail wasn't much to look at, even though he had a nice set of shoulders, but that didn't matter. She wasn't in the looking business anymore and didn't plan to start back for a long time. She had studied the three men for weeks. Quinn Lewis, along with the other two guys, was from out of state and seemed to possess a few manners. Most importantly, none of them had ever given her a second glance.

Yeah, he would do. She would have to hustle to get everything ready by Friday, but she could make it work. She continued moving the sausage around on the griddle as the list of what needed to happen over the next couple of days solidified in her mind. She looked up as the lunch whistle blew, signaling the break was ending. Several men hurried to the counter. as was normal, to grab one more dog to wolf down before returning to work. Quinn Lewis strolled away from the food truck toward the construction site, his stride long and self-assured, reminding her of Oscar, her oldest brother. Quinn turned suddenly, his chocolate eyes staring straight into hers. He smiled, and she tucked her head down. *Careful, don't draw attention to yourself now. Not when things are about to work out.*

"Ollie?"

Ollie blinked and looked up at Eric who was staring down at her. "Hmmm?"

"I asked what's the count? I've got to make a supply run this afternoon. Will the usual order get us through the rest of the week?"

"Uh." Ollie reached up and tucked a slim wisp of blond hair back in the not so beautiful hair net that clung to her head like an unwanted spider web, trapping her entire body in the life she longed to break free from. "Yeah, the normal order will do. Do you mind if I ride with you? I need to grab a couple of things before Owen picks me up this afternoon."

"Sure. We'll be going by your dad's store. Why don't I just text your brother and tell him I'll drop you off when we're done? That way, you won't have to wait for him to pick you up."

"That would be awesome." She smiled up at the mountain of a man, one of the few genuine friends she had in this town. Would he still be her friend after Friday? "Eric, thank you— for everything."

"Sure thing." He bumped his beefy arm against her bony shoulder. "You know I couldn't make it without my Ollie girl behind me a flipping and a stuffing."

Ollie looked away, shoving down the wave of guilt pushing up from her middle. She had to follow through with her plan. She had worked too long and too hard to back down now. Flipping and stuffing sausage dogs was not what she wanted to do for the rest of her life. She lifted her eyes back to the giant beside her. "Thanks, Eric."

"Anything for you, Ollie, you know that."

Chapter Two

Ollie crouched down around the edge of the old travel trailer at the end of the lot. Her legs ached from squatting for the past hour, but she forced herself to stay still. If one of the men from the surrounding trailers stepped outside and saw her, at the very least, her plan would be ruined. At the worst, well, she wouldn't go there. The sun was just peeking over the distant tree line, and lights were popping on all over the trailer park.

Lord, help me make this work. Noises had been coming from inside Floyd's little trailer for about thirty minutes, so things were going to start happening. This could go down two ways, and she would make either work. Hopefully, Quinn would unlock his truck, then go back inside. If that happened, and she prayed it did, she would hop in the backseat of his double cab truck and hide on the floorboard under her blanket. If that didn't happen, she would somehow have to get in the back of the truck before he pulled out of the lot without him seeing her. Either way, she was leaving Red Creek today. She'd never heard of Carson's Bayou, Louisiana, until Quinn Lewis had started working on the construction crew, but it didn't matter. What mattered was Carson's Bayou was not Red Creek.

Floyd's squeaky trailer door whined open, and Quinn Lewis stepped out into the gravel yard, stretching his long arms over his head. Ollie watched the man, his muscles rippling across his arms and shoulders as he looked at the dawn. Colors of purple and pink cut through the blackness. He yawned and reached his hand into his jeans pocket. Ollie pulled her hand over her mouth, stifling the yawn his actions evoked in her own body. He clicked his key fob, and the lights flickered in his truck. Great.

"You sure you want to leave?" Floyd Pearson stepped into the doorway behind Quinn. "It's not too late to change your mind."

"No, I'm heading home. I packed everything up last night except me and Rambler." Quinn opened his truck door, reached in and adjusted something in the back seat, then turned back to the man who rented him a bed. "I'm going to stop by the site and get my last paycheck, then I'm pulling out."

"Well, if I can't change your mind, I guess I better get ready for work. I don't know who I'll miss more, you or Rambler."

Ollie's leg muscles quivered as she stood, finally releasing the tension of squatting for so long. She peaked around the trailer, straining her eyes through the dim morning light. *Go inside Quinn, before it gets any brighter.*

She smiled. Quinn disappeared through the trailer door, but Floyd stepped out into the gravel. Now what? She really didn't want to ride in the back of that truck all the way to Louisiana, but if Floyd didn't get out of the way, that's what was going to happen. The older man rubbed his eyes and stretched; the sight was not nearly as enjoyable as it had been with Quinn. He turned and stepped to the opposite end of the trailer.

Taking a leak in your yard? Really? Oh well, it was now or never. Ollie slipped her ancient flip flops off. She tiptoed around the trailer through the gravel to Quinn's truck. The tiny rocks, damp with morning dew, stuck to the bottom of her calloused feet. She climbed into the backseat of the truck, wincing as a particularly sharp rock made its way into the soft flesh in the arch of her foot. She slithered across the floorboard and hunkered down behind the passenger's seat, listening as gravel crunched outside. The trailer door squeaked shut, and she held her breath. Good. Floyd must have gone back in. She looked up from the hard floorboard to the soft leather backseat above her where a duffle bag and a small ice chest sat along with a few plastic grocery bags full of chips and snacks and other things.

She eased her backpack off and adjusted it as best she could as a cushion behind her shoulders before unrolling the worn-out gray blanket she had been hugging to her chest. Pebbles still clung to the bottom of her feet, but she couldn't take the time to dust them off. She had to get out of sight before Quinn got in the truck. Hopefully, the gray lump on the floorboard wouldn't draw his attention before the cab light of the truck turned off. When he got out of the truck at the construction site, she would get the rocks off and slip her flip-flops on.

A thud hit the passenger's seat in front of her, and she held her breath. The sound of Quinn's body sliding behind the steering wheel was quickly followed by the truck door slamming shut. She swallowed, her throat dry. *I did it. I'm actually on my way. No more people looking down their noses at me, no more whispers behind my back, no more icy stares. Thank you, Lord.*

Quinn stepped out of the foreman's office, a little metal building not much bigger than a closet, and walked across the lot back to his truck. He would deposit his check in the bank on Monday. He had mailed the other ones to his sister-in-law, Esther, to deposit for him over the past few months. She wasn't nosy like his momma, who was always in his business. He opened the truck door and stared at Rambler, sitting at attention on the other side of the truck.

"What's up with you today, boy? You like riding. Why all the fidgeting?" He had fed the dog and made sure he had relieved himself before they started the trip, but on the short ride from the trailer lot to the construction site, the dog had whined and circled in the seat like something was bothering him. Quinn reached behind him and pulled a plastic grocery bag to the front. "Here." He ripped open a bag of jerky sticks and tossed one on the seat in front of him. "You can have one, but if you go to breaking wind, you won't get anything else." He patted the dog's head and tossed the bag in the back.

Quinn pulled out of the construction site and wheeled the truck around the nearby clover leaf and onto the interstate. Red Creek was in his rearview mirror, and he was headed home. He hit the playlist on his phone, and Toby Keith blared from his dashboard speakers. Nobody knew he was coming home. He wanted to stop somewhere on the way and get rid of some of this long stringy hair. When he got to his house, he would shave off the beard as well... turn back into the real Quinn Lewis, not this unkept bum he'd become over the past few months.

A few hours later, Quinn stared at his reflection in the rearview mirror. He'd been doing a lot of thinking since being in Red Creek. He'd gone out with a lot of women over the past six months, but none of them were the type of woman he wanted to settle down with. Of course, up until the past few weeks, settling down had not been on his radar. Being away from his family, away from everything familiar, made him realize how lonely he was, made him long for a little of what Drake had—a wife, kids—people who looked forward to him being home every night, and checked in on him when he was away.

Drake had talked him into going to church a few times over the past couple of years, and it had not been too bad. Laying in the lumpy little trailer bed every night, listening to Rambler snore beside him, had got him to thinking. If you wanted to catch catfish, you fished at the bottom of the pond. If you wanted bass, you didn't. If he wanted to find a woman who would make a good wife and mother, he needed to start fishing in a different pond... not the honky-tonk pond, but the church pond. He couldn't let Drake or anybody else know about why he would be going to church. He'd met a few single women from there already. They seemed nice, and not what he'd expected church girls to look like either, just normal, nice looking women. One of them was actually kind of hot.

He pulled off the interstate into a Luvs truck stop. Time to stretch, fill up with gas, and let Rambler take care of his business. He snapped the leash on the dog and walked him over to a grassy area between the rows of gas tanks and the busy road. The dog sniffed around a few minutes, then did what he had to do. Quinn poured the rest of a bottle of water he had been drinking into a Styrofoam bowl, put in the truck just for this, and let the dog drink.

"Alright boy." He opened the truck door and let the dog hop in. "Let me gas up the truck, take care of my business, then we will get back on the road. We are almost home." The dog put his paws on the back of the seat and looked over the headrest to the floorboard below. He let out a bark and wagged his tail. "I'll get you another jerky when we get on the road." The dog looked at Quinn and whined. "I'll be right back. You be a good boy, and I'll give you a treat."

Quinn pumped his gas and talked to the dog through the open window. A breeze blew his hair, and he raked his hand across his beard. It would be nice to get this extra hair off. He hurried inside and used the restroom, returning with a bag of Funyuns, a bag of jolly ranchers, and the biggest fountain Coke the place offered. They hadn't stopped for lunch, and his stomach was letting out whale calls.

"Alright boy. Let's get that jerky and hit the road. I'm gonna call in something from the Gumbo Hut and pick it up as soon as we get to Carson's Bayou. That haircut will just have to wait until tomorrow." Quinn leaned over the back seat and looked for the grocery bag. "What's that?" He didn't own a gray horse blanket. *Who's been in my truck?* He pulled on the blanket... and the blanket pulled back. "What the?"

Rambler let out a playful yelp. Quinn's eyes narrowed. He reached behind the dog and opened his glove box, taking out his pistol. He kept it unloaded, but whoever was on his floorboard didn't know that. "Alright, whoever you are, uncover yourself. I have a gun I'm getting out of my glove compartment. If you don't want to get shot, you better let me see your face and your hands."

The blanket slowly peeled back, and Quinn's eyes stretched wide. "Sausage girl?"

"No." Ollie stared up at Quinn, the gun pointed directly

at her head. "Don't call me that. My name is Olivia. Please get that gun out of my face and help me up. I'm as stiff as a poker."

"Oh." Quinn pulled the gun back as heat crept up his cheeks. *Why am I embarrassed? She's the one hiding in my truck.* "Hold on." He stuck the pistol back in the glove box as Rambler stretched further over the seat, licking the stow-away's face with his long, pink tongue. "You must not be a threat, or Rambler wouldn't take to you like he's doing."

"Or he might just like sausages." Ollie reached her hand up and took Quinn's. "I didn't have a chance to wash my hair last night, so I'm sure I still smell like the food truck." She eased up and perched on the edge of the backseat in front of Quinn's duffle bag. "Do you mind if I go to the little girl's room and grab a Coke before we hit the road? I'm about to pop."

Chapter Three

Ollie climbed out of the backseat and blew out a deep puff of air. She glanced over her shoulder as she hurried across the busy parking lot and into the Luvs station. Quinn's eyes bore into hers and she looked away. *He didn't shoot me, and he didn't kick me out of the truck. Focus on the positive.* She hurried past the long line of bathroom stalls to one near the end. Eric had probably called her dad when she didn't show up for work this morning. What could her father do? She was twenty-five, after all. It wasn't really him she was worried about. Once she got a job... and a place to live... and paid her cell phone bill so she could turn it back on... and grew a spine, she would call him and tell him where she was.

Oliver, though, how could she tell her twin that she had run out on him? Olivia and Oliver, Ollie and Ollie, so alike, but so different. She wiped her fingers across her eyes, forcing back the tears. *I will not cry. I'm strong, I'm independent.* She buttoned her jeans and stepped out of the bathroom stall, the toilet flushing automatically behind her. She stared at her face in the giant mirror under the glaring fluorescent lights. Her gray eyes, pale skin, blond hair, all colorless, boring, stared back at her. Everyone said she looked like her momma, but she didn't see it, at least not from the pictures hanging on the wall at home. Momma had run away, too, to follow a dream. *I'm not following a dream, I'm escaping a reality*.

Ollie tucked a strand of the board straight blond hair behind her ear. She washed her hands, then sniffed her fingers. At least they didn't smell like a sausage dog anymore. She stepped out of the bathroom into the truck stop and fixed a fountain drink, the eighty-nine-cent size. She looked at the M&M's but left them. Every penny counted until she got a job.

Ollie pushed open the heavy glass door with her shoulder, and her eyes scanned the gas pumps lined up across the busy parking lot. Trucks and cars filled every spot, with people of all sorts filling their tanks. Where was Quinn's truck? Her breath caught in her throat as panic caused her knees to quake. *He left me. Oh Lord, help me. I didn't think he would leave me stranded*.

"Hey."

She turned toward the familiar voice, and the pounding in her chest eased. Quinn, propped against the front fender of his truck, grinned like he found a stowaway in his truck every day. "I thought you left me," she said, walking to the truck now parked a few feet from the entrance. Rambler woofed from where he perched, half out of the open driver's side window.

"No. I'm too curious and want to find out why you hid away on my floorboard to leave you." Quinn pushed off the truck and followed her around to the passenger's door. "Rambler, backseat."

"Impressive." Ollie smiled as the dog bailed to the back and then turned around like a child, sticking his head over to the front to hear what they were saying. "He sure is a sweet boy."

"He's my best friend." Quinn looked at the drink in Ollie's hand. "Aren't you hungry? The pizza here is okay. I was gonna wait until I got home to eat, but if you want a slice of pizza, I'll get us one."

Ollie looked over at the man, smiling at her. Who was this guy? What kind of man offered to buy lunch for a woman who hitched a ride without even asking? She had pegged him for a nice guy, but was he? Nobody was that nice. Was he trying to play her? "No, I'm fine." She pushed her lips into a smile and reached for the seatbelt. "I'm just thirsty."

"Okay." Quinn shoved the door close and walked around the front of the truck. Ollie watched silently as he opened the driver's door and slid behind the wheel. He buckled in as Rambler licked his cheek. "Let's hit the road. I can drop you wherever. Do you have family near Carson's Bayou?" He pulled out of the lot and headed up the road to get back on the interstate.

"Uh." Ollie put the straw in her mouth and took a long, slow drink of the Coke. *Too far in to back out now.* She glanced out the window as they merged with the traffic flying by. "Actually, no."

"No?" Quinn's brow wrinkled, and he glanced over at Ollie. "Then where are you going?" He looked out the window at the road sign, "Skeeterville, Mississippi, five miles. Ain't that the place where that guy killed Santa Claus?"

"Is that it? I remember watching a documentary about that as a kid. My brothers scared me to death and told me Santa was dead and I'd never get another Christmas present." Ollie looked at the road sign as they flew past. "Is Carson's Bayou near here? Skeeterville sounds kind of creepy."

"We've got a little way to go." Quinn glanced over. "We're

almost out of Mississippi and in Louisiana, though. Where are you going? Somewhere in Louisiana?"

"Well, I'm going to Carson's Bayou."

"You don't have family there, so you must know people there." Quinn reached down and lifted his enormous drink from the cup holder. "Who are you going to be staying with? I've lived in Carson's Bayou my whole life. I don't know everybody, but I know a whole lot of folks."

"I thought I could stay with you." Ollie squeezed her eyelids together as Quinn spewed the mouthful of drink from his lips all over the dash. "Just for a day or two," she said, peeking out again. "I promise I'll find a place to stay in a day or two. I had to get out of Red Creek." She watched him put the drink back in the holder, ignoring that he had just showered the truck with Coke and spittle.

"Stop, Rambler." Quinn shoved the dog's head away from his face as the animal licked the soda from his beard. "Lady."

"Ollie."

"Ollie, I don't know what you were thinking was going to happen here, and I'm trying to be a gentleman about all of this—"

"And I really, really appreciate that."

"Yeah, well. Stop it, Rambler." Quinn shoved the dog again as it leaned forward, licking the drink from the dash and front seat. "You must still be thirsty." He looked from the dog to Ollie. "Grab that Styrofoam bowl down at your feet." He nodded toward the floorboard. "There's water in the cooler behind me."

Ollie picked up the bowl and leaned closer to Quinn, weaving her arm between him and the dog. *He smells good. Man, I hope he can't smell the sausage dog on me, not that it matters. It's just embarrassing is all. I've got to wash my hair.* She fished a bottle of water from the cooler and poured some in the bowl, holding it steady between them while the dog lapped it up. "I had to leave Red Creek." She looked across Rambler's head to Quinn. His eyes narrowed as he stared out the windshield at the road taking him home.

"Are you in some kind of trouble?"

"Yeah, but..." She bit her lower lip. *Lord, forgive me.* "Not with the law."

"Oh." Quinn cut his eyes down to her midsection, then pulled them back to the road. "Okay, well." He reached up and wiped a dot of Coke from his nose. "Is the father mad or something, or is your family upset?"

"They don't know." Ollie put the empty bowl back on the floorboard and reached down and fiddled with her seat belt. "They can't find out, or there'll be trouble." She stared out the window at a big green and white sign, "Carson's Bayou Exit, Forty Miles."

"I see." Quinn stared ahead for a while, not speaking. After an eternity, he glanced over at Ollie. "Alright, I'll help you, but I need you to explain a few things first."

"Okay." Ollie stared at Quinn. "I'm sorry I'm doing this to you, but I didn't have a choice."

"Who's the father? Is it one of the men from the site?"

"Eric." *Why did you say Eric, idiot? You could have made up a name, any name, but sweet Eric.* She looked Quinn in the eye, willing him to buy what she was selling.

"Your boss?" Quinn's eyes stretched. "The big sausage dog guy with all the tattoos? Will he hurt you if he finds out?"

"Yes." *God, I really am sorry. It just popped out.* A tear trickled from the corner of Ollie's eye and she sniffed. Of all the people in Red Creek, the one person who deserved her loyalty more than anyone was Eric. He had given her a job when she lost hers, and the entire town had blackballed her from practically everywhere else. He had sat by her in church and talked to her when all her old so-called friends had abandoned her.

"Look, don't cry." Quinn cut his eyes from the road to her face. "We'll figure something out. I won't kick you to the curb or anything."

"Thank you." Ollie sniffed again.

"It's just that Carson's Bayou is a very small town, even a little smaller than Red Creek. I don't know what you're expecting to find, but we are not just teaming with jobs. Are you planning on running your own food truck there? I'm not sure where you would park it to get enough money to make ends meet."

"Oh." A shudder ran down Ollie's back. "Heaven's no. If I never flip another sausage in my life, I will be happy." She wiped her eyes with the back of her hand. At least, that was the truth. Eric loved his little business. He loved being his own boss and enjoyed meeting the different people he fed. The truck had been at the hotel's construction site for months, but before that, it was in a vacant lot over by the train tracks. Eric had told her once that he showed God's love by feeding people, and every once in a while, he got to talk to a person about Jesus. A new tear escaped, and she swatted it away. *I really am a dog. Why did I hate something that my dear friend loved so much?*

"Good." Quinn turned the steering wheel to the right off the interstate and took the Carson's Bayou exit. "Look. It's gonna be okay." He fished in his pocket and pulled out his cell phone. "Do you like po' boys or fish or boudin or chicken strips or a burger? I'll order us some food. We'll be at my house in a few minutes and come up with some kind of plan."

"I've never had boudin, but any of the rest is fine." She listened as Quinn called in an order for a catfish plate and a hamburger. The little country road, lined with tall pine trees, their stiff evergreen needles pointing upward, soon turned into a road with a yellow line painted down the center. The truck pulled into a parking lot full of cars and trucks, a gray cinder block building in its center. Quinn opened his door, and the aroma of deep-fried delights caused Ollie's stomach to let out a loud, embarrassing growl. Rambler bolted over the seat into the driver's spot.

"I probably should have taken him home first, but we're here now." Quinn shoved the dog toward the middle of the truck. "I'll be right back."

Ollie reached over and wrapped her arms around Rambler's neck as Quinn disappeared inside the building. "The food's reputation must keep the place busy because it's sure nothing to look at." Rambler licked her cheek. "What am I going to do, boy? I lied about my friend and my family and about everything to Quinn. I'm trying to start over with a better life, but I'm lying like I've never learned how to speak the truth." Rambler eased his big body into her lap, nuzzling next to her. "And it's wrong. I know better." She pulled in a deep breath of courage. She would tell Quinn the truth—eventually. Just as soon as she got a job, she would tell him that Eric was a good guy, that her family was backwards and crazy, but they meant well.

Quinn stepped out the door of the cinderblock building a few minutes later, his arms full of white plastic bags. He hurried across the parking lot with long strides. "Can you hang onto him if I put this in the back seat?" he asked as he opened the truck door.

"I think so," Ollie said, tightening her arms around Rambler as he started to wiggle from one end to the other in excitement. "At least for a little while."

"We'll be home in five minutes."

Home. Ollie smiled. Rambler eased up and licked her in the face. She laughed, the sound a little loud, carrying on a little longer than it should. Would this be her home now?

"How far along are you?"

"Huh?" Ollie blinked, watching Quinn buckle his seat belt and back out of the parking lot.

"Pregnant?" Quinn looked at Ollie, then back at the road. "When's the baby due? My sister-in-law is a pediatric nurse practitioner. She can help you find a doctor for, you know, the woman stuff."

"Oh." Ollie's pale skin flushed a bright red. "I just found out—like last week." Her eyes darted around the truck. "Quinn, if you don't mind, I'd like to keep this between you and me for a while."

"Sure." Quinn smiled at Ollie. "But when you're ready, my family will help you out. They're all good people. My momma is rough around the edges, but everyone will help you out. Believe it or not, I'm the black sheep of the bunch. Lucky you, huh?"

"I think so." Ollie smiled, tenderness creeping into her eyes. "I'm sort of the black sheep, too."

Chapter Four

"I'm going to warn you." Quinn stuck the key in the front door and turned the knob. "I got the job offer that night and left early the next day, so I left everything the way it was, kind of messy." He pushed open the door, and a wave of heat hit him in the face. His upper lip pushed into his flared nostrils and the pungent aroma of dirty laundry, sour milk, dog dander, and who knew what else, wafted over him. "As a matter of fact, why don't you wait out here while I open some windows and turn on the AC?"

"I've lived with five brothers and a messy father my entire life." Ollie poked her head into the doorway and waved her hand back and forth in front of her nose. "Believe me, anything you have going on in there is not as bad as what I grew up around."

"Okay." Quinn pushed the door open wide. "Don't say I didn't warn you."

"Just point me in the direction of the bathroom, and I'm good."

"The best one is through that doorway and to the left."

What did I leave in there? A bag of dog food and Rambler's old kennel in the tub. "Let me grab you some toilet paper."

"Not necessary." Ollie reached into her backpack and pulled out a little thing of tissue as she hurried across the room. "I've got it covered."

He looked around his living room, taking in the empty pizza boxes, used solo cups scattered everywhere, a couple half full of curdled milk, dirty socks, and clothes laying here and there. A basket of clean clothes piled on a spare truck tire set in the corner, and papers and plastic bags were scattered from one end to the other. *Yeah. It's bad.* He stepped into the kitchen and laid their bags of food on the bar. The kitchen was worse than the living room. He opened the window and stuck his nose against the screen, breathing in the fresh air.

"I bumped on your air conditioning," Ollie said, stepping into the kitchen. "Want to eat first? Then we can try to get the smell out of here."

"I don't think I can eat anything with sour milk and sour feet up my nose." Quinn looked around at the filth and shook his head. "This is plumb embarrassing. I had Momma cleaning for me, but about a month before I left for Red Creek, I found her going through my bank files. She's always trying to run my business, but I didn't want to egg her on by letting her see how much was in my bank account, so I fired her."

"Why don't we open all the windows, go sit on the tailgate of your truck to eat, then do something about all this?" Ollie picked up the bag of food. "I'm pretty hungry, so I'd rather eat first and work later."

Quinn watched the woman's hips sway in her baggy jeans as she disappeared from the kitchen with their lunch. Who was this woman, and what was he going to do with her? She had looked so pitiful staring up from his floorboard, and then so scared when she stepped out the door of the truck stop and couldn't find his vehicle. Really, though, what did he know about her? *She's pregnant and feels like she can't rely on her family to help her. That's got to be tough.* One thing about the Lewis bunch, it didn't matter what pit one of them fell into or bailed off into, the family was always there to pull them out.

"You coming?" Ollie's voice called from the living room.

"Yeah, let me open the rest of the windows." Quinn took a deep breath, then gagged. *I've got to get this place in order before I decide what to do with her.* He opened another window, the one above the sink, and tied the sheer curtain in a loose knot to let the occasional breeze blow through. He hurried through the rest of the house, doing the same, then stepped outside. Ollie, sitting cross-legged on the tail of his pickup parked under the enormous water oak, waved him over. "Did you see where Rambler headed off to?"

"He came out from under your trailer, hiked his leg on the corner post of your porch, then took off across the road."

"That means Momma will know I'm home shortly." Quinn trotted down the steps and strolled the short distance to the truck. "She has a dog door on the back porch for Poochie, but Rambler goes in and out as he pleases, too."

"I bet Rambler goes in and out of everywhere as he pleases." Ollie scooted to the side, and Quinn sat on the tailgate, the Styrofoam to-go plates between them.

"Pretty much. My brother Drake won't let him inside his house when we go to town, but my nieces sneak him in a lot anyway." He picked up a plate and opened the lid. "Here, I got you the burger and fries." He passed the plate across to Ollie and picked up the next one. "I'm glad we're going ahead and eating. Cold catfish is not nearly as good as hot catfish."

"This is the biggest burger I've ever seen." Ollie lifted the burger from the plate with two hands. "No wonder that little hole in the wall does so much business."

"It doesn't have much competition, especially for lunch, but I think it would do well, anyway." Quinn grinned as Ollie took an enormous bite of the burger, her cheeks filling with food as she rolled her eyes. *I need to ask her some more questions, but I'll let her eat first. No need to get her all worked up and not be able to eat, especially being pregnant.* "Good, huh?"

"Eric let me have sausage dogs for free... or he did." A frown darkened her face for a second, then flittered away. "Let's just say, if I never eat another piece of sausage for as long as I live, I'll be fine. This burger is amazing." She took another huge bite, and her lips stretched into a broad grin. "Heaven on a bun."

"Well, the prodigal has finally come home." Mrs. Lewis stepped up to the tailgate, her skinny legs sticking out of a faded pair of blue jean shorts, soft and thin from years of washing. Her cigarette perched from the corner of her mouth. "Who's your friend?"

"Momma." Quinn set his piece of fried fish back on the plate and looked at his mother. She'd dyed her hair red while he was away. Must have been a while back because her gray roots were a good inch long. She'd always wore her hair short, cutting it herself, and applying Miss Clairol in whatever shade suited her fancy. When he left for Red Creek, she had been sporting a shade of black that didn't belong on any woman's head, especially a woman with pale skin and a slew of wrinkles from a lifetime of smoking. The fire engine red was a slight improvement. "Like your hair." He scooted off the tailgate and kissed his mother on the cheek, on the opposite side of the cigarette.

"Thank you." Mrs. Lewis reached her bony fingers into Quinn's plate and helped herself to a hushpuppy. "Honey, my name is Dolly Lewis. Since my son is low on manners and won't introduce us, I'll do it myself." Mrs. Lewis pulled the cigarette from her lips, threw her head back, and blew a long blue line of smoke. "Now, who are you and what are you doing with my son?"

"I'M OLLIE." Ollie forced herself to meet the woman's gaze and not look away. She'd dealt with too many nosy people probing into her life to let this woman make her cower. "Your son gave me a ride, and I'm paying him back by cleaning up his trailer."

"Ollie." Mrs. Lewis took a bite of the hushpuppy. "Well, Ollie, who is going to clean my son's trailer, do you have a last name?"

Uh oh. "Smith." Ollie's knee started to bounce, and she removed her plate from her lap and straightened her legs, dangling them off the truck bed. "Olivia Smith. Should I call you Mrs. Lewis or Dolly or Mrs. Dolly?"

"Mrs. Lewis will be fine for now." Mrs. Lewis's eyes traveled up and down Ollie, then she turned her stare on her youngest son. "Rambler's lost weight. I think you have too."

"We're fine, Momma. How's everything around here? Drake and his bunch doing okay? Have you heard from Hank?"

"Drake is fine. Hank called and said he might come home soon, but I'll believe it when I see it." She held her hand down and gave the last bite of the hushpuppy to Rambler who had wandered up. "I guess I'll get back across the road. You need to shave and cut that long mess." She waved her hand toward Quinn's hair. "Thanks for letting me know you made it home."

"I've barely been home ten minutes, Momma." Quinn stood up and hugged his mother. "Don't get your tail feathers ruffled. I was going to walk over and see you."

"Well." Mrs. Lewis looked down her nose at Ollie, then back to Quinn. "You mind your P's and Q's, understand? No funny business."

"Yes, ma'am."

Ollie watched the little woman walk back across the gravel road, through a large front yard. It was mostly black dirt with an occasional patch of grass, a few mud holes large enough to swim in, and scattered with dirty toys. Her wood frame house looked like it had been built in the fifties or sixties and needed a coat of paint . "Your mother is—nice."

"She has to warm up to people." Quinn sat back on the tailgate and picked up a fry from his plate. "I didn't even realize that I didn't know your last name until Momma asked."

"Sorry about that." Ollie looked down at her plate, her appetite fading away. "I saw you every day at the food truck. I guess I kind of felt like we already knew each other."

"It's not a big deal." Quinn took a bite of his fry then tossed the rest to Rambler, sitting at attention at his feet, waiting to be fed. "Smith is a common name. I think I met a Smith at the laundromat over by the sheriff's office a few weeks ago." Quinn picked up a piece of the catfish, crusty with golden cornmeal, and took a bite. "Cooper Smith was his name, I think. Is that one of your brothers?"

"No." Ollie rubbed her hand along her blue jeans. "That's a different set of Smiths." She looked over at Quinn and pushed her lips into a smile. "I'm about full. I think I'm going to go get started on your house."

"You didn't eat enough to keep a cat alive." Quinn looked at the burger and fries left on Ollie's plate. "Is the pregnancy making you nauseous? I remember my sister-in-law was sick as a dog with all three of Drake's kids."

"I guess so." Ollie slipped off the tail of the truck. "I'm

gonna stick this in your fridge and eat some more later, if that's okay."

"Yeah." Quinn took another bite of fish. "Give me about five minutes and I'll be in."

Ollie nodded. "No hurry."

"Hey." Quinn reached over and touched Ollie's arm. Her face flushed with his touch. "You don't have to do anything to pay me back for giving you a ride. Go stretch out in one of the bedrooms. Shove the junk on the floor, and take a nap. You look tired."

"No. I'm fine." She looked at Quinn's warm brown eyes. *He's going to hate me soon.* "I want to help. You've been so nice to me. I want to at least do a little something for you."

"Okay, but don't lift anything or overdo." Quinn squinted his eyes. "And in a little while we've got to talk about a few things—come up with some kind of plan to get you settled somewhere."

"That will be fine." Ollie turned and headed to the trailer, walking out of the cool shade of the oak tree into the hot summer sun. *Lord, I'm in a mess. I don't want to lie to this man, but what do I do? I don't have anywhere to go.* By now, Daddy knew she was gone. He'd probably talked to Eric and figured she'd hitched a ride out of town. It didn't matter. Nobody had seen her leave with Quinn. She hoped.

Chapter Five

"You have a problem." Ollie pulled the clean clothes from the dryer into the clothes basket and passed them to Quinn's waiting arms.

"What's that?"

"I've lived my entire life with five brothers, and I've never seen as many pairs of underwear in my entire life."

"Oh." Quinn propped up against the wall with the basket resting on his hip and watched Ollie put another load of laundry into the washer. "There's a reason for that."

"Yeah, that's what I'm afraid of." Ollie looked over her shoulder and grinned. "I'm sort of scared to ask what it is."

"I used to work offshore, home one week and gone one week."

"Yeah."

"Well, as you can tell, I'm not the neatest person around."

"You think?" Ollie snorted and poured the liquid laundry detergent into the well at the top of the fancy washing machine.

"Anyway, I wouldn't get my laundry done in time to pack back up when it was time to go to the gulf, so I'd just buy new ones to take with me." He looked at the basket on his hip crammed full of his underwear. "I guess they kind of piled up over time."

"You shouldn't ever need to buy another pair of underwear or socks as long as you live." Ollie pushed the correct buttons on the machine and turned to Quinn. "Once we wash what's in your duffle bag, you will be caught up." She looked at the basket. "Of course, we have to fold those and put them away."

"Why?" Quinn winked at Ollie. "I've never done that before."

"You also didn't keep sheets on any of your beds, but that doesn't mean you don't need them." She scooted past Quinn and walked to the living room. The sun had set a long time ago. "What time is it? Seems like we've been at this for a while."

Quinn looked at the silver watch on his arm. "It's after midnight." He dropped the clothes basket on the tan leather couch and looked around the room. "You don't mess around. This place hasn't looked this good in years." He reached down and turned on the lamp sitting on the end table. "You are a lot better at cleaning up than Momma."

"Please don't tell her that."

"I wasn't born yesterday." Quinn smiled at Ollie. "I'm getting a glass of that tea you made and some chips. You want anything?"

"No." Ollie sat on the couch and reached into the basket. "I'm fine. The washer should be filled by the time I get these folded and put away. I'm going to take a shower and hit the hay."

"Okay. I'll be right back."

Ollie watched Quinn disappear into the kitchen and sighed. She'd managed to put off his questions all evening, but it looked like the time had come. She rolled her head around on her shoulders, fatigue suddenly settling on her like a heavy fog.

"Don't worry about folding my drawers," Quinn said, stepping into the living room. "I feel kind of weird watching you do that."

"Aww." Ollie picked up a pair of the boxers and stretched them out. "Are you embarrassed?"

"Maybe." Quinn sat down on the love seat across from her. "Aren't you?"

"I've been doing men's laundry for as long as I can remember." Ollie folded the underwear, placed them on the coffee table, and grabbed the next pair. "Believe me, if you've seen one pair of boxers, you've seen them all. Nothing special about these at all. At least they're not full of holes."

"Can we talk about something else?" Quinn leaned back on the couch and looked around the room. "Please?"

"Okay." Ollie laughed. "Where's Rambler?"

"He's either on the front porch or over at Momma's. He's used to being out at night." Quinn took a drink of his tea and watched Ollie make quick work of folding the last few pieces of laundry. "Ollie, we've got to talk about what we're going to do."

"I thought you said I could stay until I get on my feet." Ollie slowly laid the last pair of underwear on the stack and looked at Quinn. *Here it comes. I need to tell him the truth, but what if he sends me back?*

"You can." Quinn set the red solo cup damp with condensation from the iced tea on the coffee table. Ollie took a coaster from the end table and slid it under the glass. "But I want you to tell me who all knew you were leaving town." He popped open the enormous yellow bag of *Lays*, and the aroma of salt and oily potatoes chips floated from the bag. "I need to know if one of these brothers you've mentioned is going to show up here and try to beat my head in for kidnapping their sister."

"Oh." Ollie's knees started to bounce, and she rubbed her hands down her legs. "Actually, I didn't tell anybody I was leaving town." She sat back on the couch and crossed her legs, then uncrossed them. "See, if I had told anyone that I was leaving, they would've asked me why."

"And you would've had to tell them you were pregnant."

"Yeah." Ollie drew the one word out into a long breath. She hadn't lied, not really. She'd agreed with what he happened to think. That's all.

"Are they looking for you now?" Quinn's eyes narrowed. "Has anybody called you or texted you wondering where you are? They must be missing you by now."

"Well." Ollie reached up and rubbed the end of her nose. "My phone isn't working, so I don't know what's going on." She swallowed and looked at Quinn, but he sat silently waiting for her to continue. "I didn't have enough money to pay my phone bill, so the company turned it off." He didn't need to know that she had scrimped and saved every penny for the past four months while she planned her escape, or how she wanted to cut off contact with her family and everyone else in Red Creek. "But you're right. They will have figured out that I'm gone."

"Don't you think we should call them?" Quinn fished a chip from the bag. "They're bound to be worried sick." He looked at Ollie's face, her eyebrows drawing together. "I won't let any of them harm you or anything. You don't need to worry about that."

"Can't we let it ride for a few days?" Ollie chewed on her bottom lip. "I don't think I can handle that kind of stress right now—you know, along with everything else."

"Alright." Quinn rubbed his ear. "I guess too much stress is not good for your baby."

"Probably not." Ollie cleared her throat and stood. She moved the stacks of underwear into the clothes basket. "I'm going to set these in your bedroom and go take a shower."

"Sure." Quinn watched her stand. "Make yourself at home. I'm going to finish my tea and then turn in."

Ollie rushed from the room, put the clothes basket at the foot of Quinn's bed, then hurried to the bedroom at the opposite end of the hall near the bathroom she had used earlier. *How long do I have before he knows I'm lying?* Ollie stared down at her front, pulling her t-shirt taunt against her blue jeans. Her hip bones stuck out of her bony frame. Three months? If she wasn't showing in three months, he would figure out the truth. What if somebody showed up looking for her before then? They wouldn't. Nobody saw her leave.

She plopped down on the edge of the bed and dropped her head in her hands. Three months to get a job, get a place to stay, and start a new life. *I've got to do this. I can't go back. I couldn't marry Jonah, not with what he was doing. Not after I knew. I didn't have a choice. I don't have a choice now.*

She listened to Quinn's footsteps as he crossed the house and stepped into the master bedroom on the other end of the hall. *I can't tell him the truth, not until I'm settled and don't have to worry about where I'm sleeping.* His deep baritone voice cut across the silent house, singing a country song about a water tower and a green heart. Her heart squeezed. *He's gonna hate me, and I don't blame him.* She stood up from the bed, and a tear trickled down her cheek. What was wrong with her? How come she couldn't have friends without hurting them? She pulled a clean t-shirt and a pair of cotton shorts from her backpack. Things would be better after a shower and a good night's sleep. They had to. They certainly couldn't be any worse.

Quinn opened his eyes and looked around. It felt odd sleeping in his own bed after so long, especially with nice clean sheets. He could get used to that. He listened to Ollie bumping around in the kitchen, humming some tune he didn't recognize. The floor felt cool to the soles of his feet as he stepped across to the bathroom. He'd take a quick shower and do something about this beard before he made an entrance.

Last night, before he went to sleep, his conscious had pricked him, making it hard to sleep. Ollie was alone. Really alone. He'd been lonely in Red Creek, but if he had needed to, he could have phoned his brothers. They would have dropped everything to come help him, no matter what kind of trouble he was in. What was it like to be part of a family that didn't care enough to have your back when you made a mistake? He and Drake didn't see eye to eye on a lot of things, but they didn't let their differences stop them from loving each other.

He'd tell her she could stay with him as long as she needed to. It was the right thing, or as Drake would say, the Christian thing to do. Quinn didn't go to church, but he wasn't a bad guy. He believed in God, and one day, when he had time, he was going to do the thing—the church thing. Even without going to church, he couldn't turn a pregnant woman out on the street.

He stepped into his bathroom and brushed his teeth, shaved off his scraggly beard, and hopped in the shower. A few minutes later, he wiped the fog from the mirror and stared at his reflection, still not looking like the Quinn he used to be. He pulled his hair back to the nape of his neck and put in a rubber band to hold the brown strands out of his face. If he didn't get to the barber today, he would whack it off with his pocketknife. If not, Momma would try to stick a bowl on his head and cut it like when he was a kid.

The front door opened and shut while he finished getting ready, and he strained to hear who had entered his house. Probably Momma. Maybe she wouldn't harass Ollie too much before he could get in there. He opened his bedroom door and stepped through the hall into the living room, pulling a clean white t-shirt over his head as he went.

"Look what the cat drug in." Drake stepped into the living room from the kitchen with a cup of coffee in his hand.

Quinn looked at his brother and grinned. "Doesn't anybody in this family ever knock?"

"You don't," Drake said, slapping him on the back. "Why should I? Congratulations, little brother."

"Thank you," Quinn said, only half listening. He watched Ollie walk up behind Drake, her hair tousled from sleep. Her t-shirt and shorts were wrinkled from where she had slept in them. She didn't look at Quinn, but hurried over to the couch and started straightening the pillows she had put there last night. *She really is amazing.* He'd mopped the floors, refusing to let her do the heavy stuff, but she had worked like a dynamo, not slowing down until the entire house looked and smelled clean. She'd even made him move the furniture to vacuum, which was a good thing. He found a box with half a pizza shoved under the love seat and about eight dirty socks under the couch and gobs of wadded up plastic wrappers from old jolly ranchers. "Are you by yourself?"

"Yeah." Drake looked from Quinn to Ollie, then back at Quinn. "Esther took the kids to something at the library. Momma called a few minutes ago and said you were home, so I decided to run over." Drake took a sip of his coffee and shook his head. "Is that all you are going to say? Thank you?"

Quinn pulled his eyes from Ollie, whose back was still to

him. She hurried to the window and started opening the mini blinds. "Oh, sorry." His eyes narrowed at Drake, who was staring at him with a ridiculous grin on his face. "I thought you two had already met."

"We have." Drake chuckled. "How do you think I found out the good news? You know not much surprises me, but when Ollie there told me you two were married, I didn't know what to say."

Quinn cut his eyes from his brother, still standing there with a sappy grin on his face to Ollie, her back suddenly rod straight and as still as a statue. "Yeah." He looked back at Drake. "I don't really know what to say, either."

Chapter Six

Ollie's gut clenched in a knot, and she closed her eyes, waiting for Quinn to explode, tell his brother she was lying, demand she leave his house. She hadn't intended to lie to Drake, but what was she supposed to do? He had barged into the kitchen unannounced while she was fishing the sugar off the top shelf of the pantry, her arms stretched over her head, her midsection showing. He caught her completely off guard. She looked like she just crawled out of bed, which she had, but not Quinn's bed, or at least not out of bed with Quinn. It didn't matter, though. She could tell by the way Drake had looked at her he was jumping to a conclusion that was showing her in an awful light.

"Where's Quinn?" He had reached up and retrieved the sugar and handed it to her.

"He hasn't gotten up yet."

"I'm his brother, Drake. Who are you?"

"Ollie."

"Ollie? Do you have a last name?"

His tone had not been like Quinn's mother, not condescending, but extremely curious. "Lewis. I'm Quinn's wife."

Why had she said that? She hadn't even attempted to tell this man the truth. Nope, just lied from the get-go like a lazy dog in the shade. If he hadn't looked at her with what? Compassion, like it saddened him to see her in his brother's house. If he had looked down his nose at her like his mother had, she probably wouldn't have lied. No, if he had snubbed her, she would have puffed up and put him in his place. That was for sure. She had done that so many times in the past that it was like her second nature. The way this guy looked at her, though, made her want him to think good about her. It was like she didn't want to let him down even though he was a complete stranger—and she had lied.

"How long have y'all been married?" Drake asked from behind her, pulling her thoughts back to the present.

Ollie opened her eyes and stared out the window into the yard where Rambler and an enormous black poodle lounged under the oak tree. No need to cower down now. If Quinn threw her out on her ear, she had nobody to blame but herself, her stupid, lying self.

"Ollie?" Quinn's hand touched her shoulder, and she jumped. "Why don't you fill Drake in on the details?" He squeezed her shoulder, his tone full of sarcasm, or at least it sounded that way to her. "You remember them so much better than I do."

"I..." Ollie turned and looked up into Quinn's face. The open, warm smile that had been there last night was gone. He smiled, but this smile was the smile you put on when you wanted to throttle someone, but you were too polite to air your dirty laundry in public. She had gotten that smile a few times over the years from her father when she let her tongue get the best of her. "Um." She stepped back, the cool metal mini blinds poking into her back. "I really need to go get dressed."

"That's okay." Drake set his coffee cup on the end table by

the love seat. "I've got to be going, anyway. Why don't you two come over for supper tonight, and you can tell me and Esther all about it? She will be dying to hear how you trapped my brother into tying the knot."

"I don't know." Ollie's eyes darted from Quinn, still staring at her, too close for comfort, to Drake. "I have a lot I need to do."

"I won't take no for an answer." Drake stepped over and slapped his brother on the back again. "The woman that is able to snag my little brother's heart has to be something special. We want to get to know you better." He grinned. "Besides, you're family now." He looked from Ollie to Quinn. "Walk me to my truck. I want to talk to you about a job you might be interested in. That's why I was stopping by, but when Ollie here told me the good news, I completely forgot about it."

Ollie watched the brothers walk out the front door then hurried to the bedroom. She shoved the few things she had unpacked the night before into her backpack. Should she write him a note and explain that she was sorry? She could lay it on the bar in the kitchen and leave out the back while he was out front talking to his brother. No, she obviously was a liar, but she wouldn't sneak out like a complete coward. She still had a sliver of dignity.

She threw on her jeans from yesterday and slipped the backpack on her shoulders. She would apologize, thank him for the ride and the bed for the night, then hit the road. He could tell his brother she was crazy. He probably thought she was, anyway. It was time to throw in the towel and move on. At least she was out of Red Creek. She slid her feet into her flip-flops and hurried into the living room.

"Going somewhere?" Quinn sat on the couch; arms crossed over his chest. "And if you don't mind, I'd like a straight answer."

Quinn stared at Ollie standing in the doorway, rubbing her hands together. *She's nervous. Good. Serves her right.* "I told Drake we couldn't make it tonight."

"Thanks."

"I also told him to keep our nuptials to himself. That I wanted to let Momma know before the word gets around town that I'm married." He stared.

Ollie bit her lower lip, her eyes scanning the room. "Look. I think it's better if I go. I've already complicated your life enough with all my—stuff."

"You're probably right." Quinn rubbed his hand across his freshly shaven jaw. "But here's the deal. I don't know how it is where you come from, but around here, gossip travels fast. If somebody sees you walking through Carson's Bayou, word will get back to Drake." He watched her shift the straps of the backpack on her shoulders, still not looking at him. "And when word gets back to my brother that my little wife is running away from her new husband. Well..."

"Nobody knows me around here. They wouldn't know I'm your—wife."

"See. You're missing the point here." Quinn pulled his shoulders back into the sofa, stretching. He needed to do something to work this tension out. Tension had never been an issue for him until yesterday. "The fact that nobody knows who you are is the problem. Everybody knows everybody around here. And if they don't recognize you, they will make it their business to get to know you. A strange woman walking through town will start tongues a wagging for sure."

"Oh." Ollie finally looked at Quinn. Her shoulders

drooped like a melting fudgesicle. "I've really messed things up. He was just so nice, not judgie like your..."

"Momma?" Quinn smiled, then quickly recovered his stern glare. *Let her squirm. Maybe she'll think twice before she lies to and about me again.* "Drake hasn't always been." Quinn's eyes softened. "If there's anybody in town who knows what it's like to be down on your luck, it's Drake. My brother and I have sewed our wild oats, but Drake had some things happen to him that would have crushed a lot of people. Things that were completely out of his control. It changed him. Made him..." Quinn's brow pulled down. "I'll just say that if there's anybody in this town who you could have shared you situation with and them not judge you, it's Drake."

"Boy." Ollie blew out a huff of air and looked up at the ceiling. "I guess I blew that one then." She walked over and fell onto the love seat across from Quinn. "What do we do now?"

"We?" Quinn raised an eyebrow. "I'm going to go get a haircut." He sat forward. "What you do is up to you, but you are welcome to tag along."

"You—don't hate me?"

"There are very few people that I hate, Ollie." Quinn stood up. "It's a waste of time and energy. But I do need you to make me a promise."

Ollie slipped her backpack off her shoulders. "Anything."

"Before you make any more grand, life-changing announcements that include me, let me in on them first."

"I will, Quinn." Ollie stood, bobbing her head up and down. "I was stupid. I promise, I won't be again. Let me put my things up. I'll be right back."

Ollie hurried out of the room, and Quinn frowned. *It's time I learned a little more about who you are, who you really are.* He pulled his phone from his jeans pocket and scrolled down until he found Floyd Pearson's number.

> Have you filled my spot yet?

He couldn't come right out and ask Floyd about Ollie, or Floyd would be suspicious. He looked at the far wall where Ollie was bumping around on the other side in the bedroom. Until he knew what was really going on with his house guest, he'd keep her connections with him a secret. She lied to Drake easily enough. Chances were she had lied to him about a few things, too.

"I'm ready." Ollie stepped into the living room and smiled. "Do you mind if we stop by the grocery store on the way back? I'm a pretty decent cook, but you need a few supplies."

She's definitely quick on her feet. Quinn slipped his phone in his pocket. "Yeah. I need to buy dog food, anyway." He stood up and followed her to the truck, locking the front door behind him. His phone buzzed in his pocket, and he stood outside the truck door, fishing it out.

> Yeah. But this guy snores so loud he shakes the whole trailer. You sure you don't want to come back?

> No, I'm needed around here for a while. I do miss the sausage dogs from the food truck.

> Dude! There was a big stink after you left. Sausage girl disappeared. Cops came to the work site and everything.

Now we're getting somewhere.

> What happened to her?

Quinn looked through the truck door window at Ollie. She was staring at him. Let her stare. If she wouldn't be honest with him, he'd find out what was going on with her by other means.

> The police aren't sure. She left some rich guy at the altar about eight months ago. They are asking around. They must think that guy has something to do with it.

Quinn glanced back up at Ollie and smiled. So, she left a guy at the altar, then hopped into the sack with her boss at the food truck, and now she was pregnant. No wonder lying to Drake hadn't been a big deal.

> Sounds like I left just in time.

> No, man. We're all working as usual. It just gives us something to talk about besides football.

Quinn hit the thumbs up sign and shoved his phone in his pocket.

"Was that Drake?" Ollie asked, watching Quinn slide behind the wheel of the truck. "Is he asking questions?"

"No." Quinn started the truck and pulled onto the gravel road. "That was a friend. Drake will tell Esther, his wife, what's going on, but he won't try to get into my business. Not much, anyway." He pulled his truck into the gas station on the way into town. "I've got to get gas. You want a Coke?"

"Yeah, but I'll go in and get it." Ollie unbuckled her seatbelt and climbed out the passenger's side door.

Quinn's eyes followed Ollie into the store as he pumped the gas. Ollie stepped up to the counter, and the guy who owned the place appeared from the back. *What's she talking to Ed about?* She opened the store door a few minutes later as he was replacing the nozzle in the gas pump. "Everything okay?"

"Yeah." Ollie climbed back into the truck and smiled at Quinn. "I've got a job."

"You're going to work here?" Quinn wrinkled his brow. "For Ed?"

"It can't be any harder than the food truck."

"I guess not." He pulled out of the lot and headed across town to the barbershop.

"Don't worry. You won't have to drive me to work. Ed said he would come pick me up."

"Yeah." Quinn opened his truck door. "I bet he did. Ollie, Ed's a sleaze. He's only been married seven times. The past three were to women who started out working for him in that store."

"Oh." Ollie lifted her chin. "Well, that's not going to happen to me. Don't worry."

"Because you're already married to me," Quinn said, his lips pushing into a thin line. "Remember?"

"Oh, yeah. I forgot."

Chapter Seven

"**A**re there any churches close by?" Ollie flipped the bacon sizzling in the cast-iron skillet with a fork, not turning to look at Quinn as he poured his morning coffee. Last night she made her daddy's favorite meal, chicken and dumplings. She learned to make it in junior high from Aunt Sadie, her daddy's older sister who lived next door.

"You can feed a lot of hungry men with one bird, Ollie, if you know what you're doing," Aunt Sadie would often say. "Since it looks like your daddy is determined to remain single for the rest of his days, it's going to be up to you to help keep all them brothers of yours fed."

Aunt Sadie had helped turn Ollie into a cook and house-keeper while other girls her age were trying out for cheer-leading or joining school clubs or playing sports. "We all have to pitch in and get you young'uns raised. It sure doesn't look like your momma is ever coming back to do it. I don't know why that brother of mine keeps hanging on to that hare-brained idea."

Quinn ate his fill of the meal and thanked her when he

was done. Afterwards, she had hurried to her bedroom, scared he would try quizzing her about her plans or her past or all of the other details of her life she was trying to avoid sharing with him. She beat him out of bed again the next morning, but thankfully no unannounced family members dropped by.

"There are several churches in town." Quinn stepped up to the refrigerator and pulled out a jug of milk. "That's one thing that's not in short supply around here."

"Would you mind if I..." Ollie felt Quinn standing beside her and turned. A flutter caught in her chest as he leaned over and opened the cabinet, his arm brushing against hers. *If I had known how good looking he was under that scraggly beard and long hair, I never would have climbed in his truck.* She took a step over, giving him room to maneuver without making further contact. "Would you mind if I borrow your truck to go to church today? I'll go straight there and straight back. Or you can let me ride with you if you're going."

"You want to go to church?" Quinn stared at Ollie as he pulled the glass from the cabinet.

"Yes." Ollie's eyebrows pulled low. "What's wrong with that?"

"I just." Quinn turned his gaze to the milk jug. "Never mind."

"No." Ollie turned from the stove, her hands on her hips. "You can say it. What's a woman who has stowed away in the back of a stranger's truck and then lied about being married doing wanting to go to church?"

"There's that." Quinn opened the fridge and replaced the milk. "And the fact that you're pregnant — and not really married."

"Yeah, I know that." Ollie lifted the piping hot, crispy bacon from the skillet and tossed it on the plate lined with a paper towel to absorb the grease. "That doesn't mean I can't go to church." She picked up the plate of bacon and turned. "Do you think I'm not good enough to go to your church?" She slammed the plate on the bar and glared at Quinn. "Because if that's the case, I can go to a different one. It doesn't have to be the one you go to."

"Oh, no." Quinn held up his palm. "You can go to any church you want to. I don't care at all." He took a sip of his coffee and set his mug down by his glass of milk. "Forget I said anything."

Ollie turned back to the stove and slipped on an oven mitt. *Why am I so defensive with him? I'm biting the hand that's feeding me.* She reached into the oven and pulled out a pan of biscuits. She turned and set them on a trivet on the bar. "Look. I'm sorry. Last year some things happened, and when I went to church afterwards, a few people weren't very nice." She pulled the mitt from her hand and shrugged her shoulders. "I guess I'm just a little touchy, but I need to go to church. Every time I do the stupid stuff I do, I ask God to forgive me." She looked up at Quinn, staring at her. She tucked a strand of blond hair behind her ear. "I know what I did wasn't right, but I'm forgiven, and I want to go worship." Her voice softened. "How can I grow and get more like Christ if I don't go learn about Him?"

"It's okay," Quinn said, his voice losing the hard, business like edge it had before. "You can go to any of the churches you want." He reached down and picked up a piece of the bacon. "I'm not the churchgoing type, and I assumed you weren't either. I guess I was wrong."

"I couldn't make it without God." Ollie reached up and rubbed her fingers down the side of her cheek. "Most of the time I feel like I'm the dumbest, most sinful child that God has, but if I didn't have my faith in Him, I couldn't make it through."

"You know what?" Quinn bit off a piece of the bacon. "I

think I'll go to church with you." His eyes twinkled. "The roof might fall in on our ears, and my brother will probably pass out cold when I walk in, but hey, why not?"

"Are you sure?" Ollie asked. "Because I don't mind going by myself."

"I'm sure." Quinn reached over and stuck his fork under one of the biscuits. A curl of steam rose from the pan as he lifted it and plopped it on his plate. "I'd been thinking about going to church before I left Red Creek."

"I really am sorry I bit your head off a few seconds ago. You've been good to me, and I have no right to be snappy to you."

"Don't worry about it. I imagine most pregnant women get that way."

"Yeah." Ollie bit her lower lip and turned her back to Quinn. "I guess so." *Lord forgive me.*

Quinn sneaked a peek over at Ollie again for the tenth time as everyone bowed their heads. One thing was certain, she hadn't been lying about what she said earlier this morning. They arrived at Drake's church a few minutes late for what the website called corporate worship. "What does that mean, corporate worship?" Quinn had asked as Ollie looked up the information on his phone. *She needs a phone. Everybody has a phone, even Momma.* "That sounds like some kind of fancy board meeting."

"That's another name for preaching." Ollie had flipped her hair over her shoulder and scrolled down the screen. "I've always called it big church." She cut her eyes over to Quinn. "So, you've truly never been to church?"

"I've been." Quinn lifted his chin. "I went to a few of their parties after the football games when I was in high school, and that school thing they have for the kids every summer." He had breathed in the honeysuckle scent from her hair. *That does smell nicer than sausage.* "I just never made it to this part."

"Here it is." Ollie stopped scrolling and pointed to the phone screen. They start at eleven but are planning on doing two services soon. "Let's get there about five minutes late. That way, we can sneak in without everybody looking at us."

They followed her instructions and slipped in the door and sat on the back pew where a sign read, "reserved for first-time visitors." Apparently, the sneaking in late thing was common knowledge among the church crowd.

He had looked around the church with its high ceilings, rows of pews, and the stage up front with a giant screen behind it. A couple of guys played guitars, and Drake's son's piano teacher was on a keyboard. There were even drums. Their light bill was probably sky high because it was so cold you could have hung meat in the place. Everyone was standing, singing something about God being holy. Ollie slipped into the pew ahead of him and immediately started singing along.

The hour passed by quicker than he'd expected. He'd listened to what the preacher said, nothing he didn't agree with, really. He just hadn't given God or anything about Him a ton of thought. He was a busy man, trying to live a decent life. God would get more attention one day when things slowed down.

The person who kept his attention had been Ollie. He couldn't help it. His eyes wouldn't stop looking. She hadn't noticed, and that was what was amazing. Ollie was a fidgeter. He'd picked up on that when she'd got in the front of his truck the day they met. If her eyes weren't moving from place to place, some part of her body seemed to be. It was cute, but very obvious.

Not here, not in this freezing cold building crammed with strangers. She sang the songs and listened to the preaching with complete focus, like her life depended on it or something. Drinking it in. That's what it looked like. The only time she'd really lost that hungry, absorbing gaze had been when the preacher instructed them to pray, and she closed her eyes.

He'd studied her from the corner of his eye the first time the guy up front leading the music told everyone to bow their heads. That was right after the first song ended. She hadn't seemed to listen to what the man up front was saying in his prayer. Her lips had moved silently, her eyes squeezed shut, but her face had been packed with emotion. *She really is talking to God.* His eyes had darted around the room, quiet except for the man up front asking the Lord to bless their time together with Him. It was hard to see many from their back row spot. Most of the people just had their eyes closed and seemed to be listening. When they sat down, Ollie had pulled a tissue from a box on the seat beside her and dabbed her eyes.

What was her deal? She could lie to him and his brother without batting an eye. Her head was as hard as a goat's, and she seemed to have no idea how to stay out of trouble. What in the world did she get from—this?

After the service, as the preacher had come down from the stage, they had prayed again. Some people were going to the front to pray with him. Quinn had closed his eyes but suddenly felt a bump on his arm. He looked over at Ollie, nudging him to move out into the aisle. No, she could go down front if she wanted to, but he was staying right where he was. He closed his eyes, but she bumped him harder. He looked over. She glared at him, her lips in a flat line, jaw firm, the old Ollie back. He glared back and shook his head. *I'm not budging on this, woman. I might play around with a lot of things, but I don't plan on getting on God's bad side today, not even for you.*

She stretched her eyes even wider and poked her lips out. Thank goodness they were in the back row, and everyone had their eyes closed or they would have been drawing attention. He glared back, but she ignored him, squeezing past. Instead of heading to the front where the preacher waited, she walked to the back and slipped out the door.

Oh. Okay. He could do that. He stepped into the aisle and looked around sheepishly as he started toward the door. Drake, several rows ahead and across the aisle, looked his way, grinning like he had just won the lottery. *Well, I'll never hear the end of this now.*

Chapter Eight

Monday morning Ollie looked at herself in the bathroom mirror, hair slicked back in a tight ponytail, not a lick of makeup on. Her gray eyes stared back at her like an owl, large and round in her thin face. She rubbed her finger over her lips. Nothing to see here. Even if Ed was a flirt like Quinn said, he wouldn't give her a second glance. She stepped over to the bed and grabbed her purse. She had taken her get away money out and shoved it under the mattress, leaving herself ten dollars to make it through the day. She tucked her pink gingham blouse, faded from too many washings, into her brown cargo shorts. She slipped her feet in her flip-flops and looked down at her toenails naked without polish.

When was the last time she'd been concerned about her looks, especially her feet? Well, she had worried about her looks a lot since *that day*, but not in the normal way, the way she used to. Ever since she'd walked away from Jonah, actually run away from him, she'd done everything she could to fade into the background, to disappear from the notice of everyone around her. Of course, that plan had backfired, like most everything she'd done in Red Creek. People talked, and leaving Jonah Blue at the altar was a big deal, an enormous deal. Instead of disappearing from everyone's radar like she'd hoped, her change in appearance had put an unexpected spin on the gossip surrounding her very public jilting of the town's golden boy.

"She's let herself go, poor girl. I'm sure she's regretting leaving him like she did."

She'd tried to ignore the two ladies talking about her after she walked past them at the grocery store a couple of weeks after the wedding fiasco, the day that had started her fall from grace. She'd heard several spins to her tale. Some said she'd fled the church because she'd suddenly realized she wasn't good enough to marry a Blue. Others said she broke it off because she was secretly in love with someone else. A few felt she left him at the altar because she'd discovered that he was secretly in love with someone else, but was too noble to break it off with her. Yeah, the old birds had spun it several different ways. The one that had hurt the most was when she heard from her twin that people were saying she was suicidal, and her dad was keeping her locked up at home so she wouldn't hurt herself.

She didn't care what everyone thought. Well, yes, she did. She tried not to, but being the doormat for the entire town had taken its toll. Not just on her, but on her entire family. After the almost wedding, she'd hidden out at home for two weeks, not going anywhere. She'd lost her job the day she'd jilted the boss's son, so she'd had no place she'd needed to be. Going from a social butterfly to the town hermit had not gone unnoticed. When Oliver told her what everyone was saying, that she was trying to kill herself, she'd stiffened her spine and re-entered the world.

Ollie pushed the painful thoughts aside. She grabbed her purse from the bed and slipped it on her shoulder. Today was not the day to wallow in self-pity. She couldn't redo her past. She had moved on—literally. It was time to move on emotionally, too. She stepped out of her bedroom, turning off the light, and closing the door. Ed was supposed to be by to pick her up at nine. She had ten minutes to kill. Time for a cup of coffee and a left-over biscuit.

"Are you sure you want to go through with this?"

Ollie dropped her purse on the corner of the bar and pulled a coffee mug from the cabinet. Quinn was perched on a barstool, a plate with a half-eaten biscuit, a thick slice of yellow cheese, and a puddle of syrup in front of him. "Yes." She grabbed a pod for the fancy coffee maker from the box sitting near the toaster and shoved it into the machine. "I've got to get a job and, like you said, there aren't a lot of them around for folks like me—with limited skills."

"Well, if you're determined to work for Ed, then I'm going to drive you there."

"That's not necessary." Ollie reached in the refrigerator and grabbed the half and half. "He'll be here in a few minutes to get me." She pulled her cup of steaming coffee from the Keurig and started doctoring it. "I've got it all worked out."

"Nope." Quinn dabbed the corner of his biscuit in the puddle of golden syrup. "I don't think you should work for the man, but if you are, we are going to set some ground rules."

"We?" Ollie put her hand on her hip. "*We* don't have a say so in this." She stirred her coffee and turned, dropping the spoon in the sink. "I can handle Ed whatever his last name is. Believe me, I've dealt with his kind before. I will be fine. Besides, this is my problem, not yours."

"It became my problem when you told my brother we were married." Quinn dipped the corner of the biscuit in the syrup again. "Any man with any sense would not let his wife work for Ed Duchant. I don't plan on being the laughingstock of every Tom, Dick, and Harry in the parish because they saw my wife riding around with the town's greasy old Casanova."

"I didn't peg you for the type of person who cared what people thought." Ollie lifted her mug to her lips, her eyes down. She'd been on the other side of a similar conversation last year with her father. A twinge of guilt ran through her middle, but she ignored it. She hadn't intended to put Quinn in the middle of her mess, but now he was. "Ignore them. Believe me, gossip won't kill you, or I'd be dead and buried."

"I don't care what people say, but it doesn't hurt to use your brain, Ollie. I don't have a job right now either. I'm not hurting, but I do plan on going back to work soon. Drake wants me to go in with him, be a welder's apprentice until I learn the job. When I do, I will have to deal with all these people around here on a daily basis. It's going to be bad enough when word gets out we're married. Then when folks find out we're not married, well—I need to keep at least a shred of a decent reputation so people will hire me. Plus, I have my brother's reputation to think of. I'm not backing down on this, so you might as well give in."

A horn blew outside, and Quinn stood up from the bar. "Finish your coffee. I'll tell Ed you will be at the store in a few minutes."

Ollie watched Quinn disappear out the front door. Lies. They always did the same thing. They leached out of her life into the lives of the people around her, poisoning everything they came into contact with. "Lord, help me. I don't want to be this way. I want to be honest, God, I do, but I need a place to live and a job. I don't have a choice."

She poured the rest of her coffee down the drain and snatched up her purse. *Trust the Lord with all your heart and lean not to your own understanding.* The memory verse popped into her head, and she closed her eyes, wincing at the answer to her prayer. She would tell Quinn the truth about everything soon. As soon as her life straightened out.

"You don't have to work here." Quinn watched Ollie unbuckle the seat belt. "We can ask around and find you a better job. The Presbyterian church has a daycare. Why don't you tell Ed you've changed your mind? We can run by the church, and you can talk to them."

"No. This is going to work." Ollie looked over at Quinn and smiled. "This is only twenty-four hours a week. Maybe we can go by the daycare too. I might can work both places."

"I guess so. If you don't think it will be too hard on you with the baby."

"No." Ollie looked down and smoothed out a wrinkle on her shirt. "I'm sure it will be fine. I really need the money so I can start looking for my own place."

"Okay. Well."

Ollie reached over and patted Quinn's hand. "I'm a big girl, Quinn. If he tries to get frisky, I'll put him in his place."

Like you did Eric? Quinn looked away, pushing down the thought before he said something he shouldn't.

Ollie opened her door and slid out of the truck. "I'll see you in six hours."

He watched her walk through the glass doors to where Ed waited, a slimy grin on his face. He wanted to follow her in and knock that grin right down Ed's throat, but Ollie would throw a hissy-fit if he did. He jerked his truck into gear and sped out of the parking lot. He hurried through town, pulled up in front of Drake's house, and walked around back to where Drake's work truck was parked.

"You ready to hit the road?" Drake stepped out of the metal shed nearby. "We've got a busy morning. I've already been hard at it since six. You are gonna have to give up these banker's hours if you want to work with me."

"I know." Quinn opened up the passenger door of Drake's work truck. He set a toolbox behind the seat and threw a pair of leather work gloves on the dash. "I had to drop Ollie by her job this morning, but I'll figure everything out and be here early tomorrow."

"She's already got a job?" Drake picked up the gloves from the dash and dropped them on the seat beside him. "Your new wife is a real go-getter. Where's she working?"

"At Eds." Quinn looked out the dirty windshield.

"At the gas station?" Drake stared across the truck at his brother. "Why in the world are you letting her work there?"

"Letting her?" Quinn rolled his eyes. "I don't let her do anything. Believe me."

"Trouble in paradise?" Drake chuckled and cranked the truck. "Don't worry. She looks like the type of woman who can handle herself." Drake picked up his insulated mug from the cup holder and took a drink. "She got you to church yesterday, so it looks like she can handle you, too."

"I had already made up my mind to start going to church while I was away working." Quinn slumped down in the seat. He appreciated Drake helping him get this job and teaching him, but it was going to be a long day... a long week.

The morning passed by faster than Quinn expected. After Quinn had sat silently sulking for the first five minutes, Drake had mercifully changed the subject from Ollie to his kids. They rode for an hour to a construction site, and Quinn watched his brother work on the steel girders of a bridge. It would one day replace the old rusty one a few yards away where the noise of the traffic made it impossible to hear anything around them. That worked for Quinn. He wasn't in a talking mood today, anyway.

His phone buzzed, and he stepped away from where Drake stooped over the metal beam, the blow torch hot in his hand. He lifted the gray helmet away from his face and fished his phone from his pocket. He clicked the ignore button. He would call Momma back when he could hear her.

> Have you lost your ever-loving mind?

Quinn looked at the text from his mother. *Well, I guess she found out about Ollie's job.*

> Can't talk now. At work with Drake. Lot of noise. Explain later.

It was going to be a long afternoon.

Chapter Nine

Quinn pulled into the gas station and walked up to the front door. The idea of Ollie working with Ed had eaten at his gut all day. On the drive back into town with Drake, he decided to stop by the man's place and give him another talking to. He had told Ed he didn't want any funny business with his new wife this morning, but the oily scoundrel had laughed and told him he had nothing to worry about. Yeah. Right.

Locked. That's odd. He peered through the glass into the darkened store, but the place seemed deserted. Ed was supposed to drop Ollie back at the trailer when she was done with her shift, but the store stayed open until after dark. Quinn hadn't liked Ollie riding home with Ed, but he had to work, too. *I could have let her use the truck.* He rubbed his hand across his neck and hurried back to his truck. If that sleaze ball did something to Ollie, he'd break every bone in his body. He should have let her use his truck. Why hadn't he gotten her a cell phone?

He broke the speed limit leaving town, and slung gravel

everywhere, turning onto their dead end road. The trailer looked empty and Rambler was nowhere in sight, but his feet flew through the house. "Ollie?" The place was quiet as a tomb. He jumped as the phone vibrated in his pocket.

"Momma, have you talked to Ollie?" He heard the anxiety in his voice, but he didn't care. This woman was living in his house, was his responsibility—sort of.

"Come on over. She's teaching me how to make a dump cobbler."

"She's with you?" Quinn pulled in a deep breath. "What's she doing with you?"

"If you would have answered your phone when I called like a good son should, you would know. Come on over. Supper's about ready."

The phone went dead. Quinn pulled it from his ear and stared at the screen. Why was he so stink'n mad? Ollie was okay. That's what he wanted. If she had listened to him in the first place and never went there this morning, he wouldn't be all worked up now. He grabbed a can of Coke from the refrigerator and tromped into the yard. The sun was setting, and katydids called out in the near darkness. Purple hues with deep orange feathers streaked the sky. A faint breeze touched his skin, and he breathed in the scent of the wisteria growing wild in the trees. He walked across the road, his steps slow, letting the peacefulness of the evening take away his anger. A rain frog called, and another one answered.

He stepped onto his momma's front porch, the house he had lived his teen years in. Drake had bought the place from his momma when he got married the first time to Paige. When he married Esther and moved to her house in town, his momma had bought the house back. "Hey, boy." Quinn reached down and scratched Rambler behind the ears. He emptied the last few drops from the Coke can and entered his mother's house.

Women's laughter floated from the kitchen, and Quinn frowned. When did they become big buddies? The aroma of fried chicken caught his nose, and his stomach growled.

"How was your first day?" Ollie stepped from the kitchen into the living room and smiled at Quinn. She tilted her head to the side. "What's wrong?"

"I went by the gas station, and the place is closed." Quinn flopped down on the love seat and crushed the Coke can with his fist. "What happened? Did Ed do something? Is he in jail?"

"Calm down." Ollie eased down on the couch across from Quinn. "I told you I could handle Ed."

"So something did happen." The vein on the side of Quinn's temple throbbed. "I never should have left you there this morning."

"Would you hush a minute?" Ollie glared at Quinn like he had done something wrong.

"I'm listening." Quinn crossed his arms over his chest. "What happened?"

"Ed got a little—frisky." Ollie held her hand up as Quinn sat forward. "Hold on and let me finish. He got into my personal space, and I punched him in the nose."

"You? Punched him?" A smile crept across Quinn's face. "I bet that was a first."

"He bled like a stuck pig."

"If you would have answered your phone, I would have told you already." Quinn's momma stepped from the kitchen, wiping her hands on a dish towel.

"It was too noisy to understand you, Momma." Quinn looked back at Ollie, and his eyes crinkled with laughter. "You socked ole greasy Ed in the nose. What did you do? Use the store phone and call Momma to come pick you up?" His brow creased. "How did you get her number?"

"No." Mrs. Lewis stood by the edge of the couch. She laid

her hand on Ollie's shoulder. "I picked the poor girl up from the side of the road. Quinn, I can't believe you are treating your new bride this way. I raised you better."

"What did I do?" Quinn's eyebrows lifted, and he stared at his mother and then Ollie. "Did you tell her I didn't want you working there?"

"I told her." Ollie smiled as she reached up and patted Mrs. Lewis's hand. "Several times."

"If you'd wanted to, you could have stopped her." Mrs. Lewis pushed her lips out. "I can't believe my daughter-in-law was walking home by herself after defending herself from the town moron."

Quinn leaned his head back and stared at the ceiling. He raised his head and looked at both women. His mother looked down her nose. Ollie grinned. *She knows good and well this is not my fault.* "Momma, I told her not to work there. She's got a head as hard as a brick wall."

"Quinn Lewis." Mrs. Lewis put her hands on her hips. "I won't have you speaking to this poor girl that way, especially after the day she's had. Not in my house."

"I'm going home." Quinn stood from the couch. "You two enjoy each other's company."

"Quinn." Ollie stood and placed her hand on his arm. "Don't go. You must be hungry."

Quinn looked down, the touch of her hand burning his skin. "I'm starved."

"Come on." She squeezed his arm, and the heat of her touch moved up to his chest. "Let's eat, then we can walk home together." She looked back at Mrs. Lewis. "He really did try to stop me, and I wouldn't listen."

"Come on, son." Mrs. Lewis's eyes softened. "Ollie fried the chicken and the okra. It will be nice to eat someone else's cooking for a change, and I want you to tell me how your first day of working with your brother went." Mrs. Lewis looked at

Ollie. "My other daughter-in-law is not that good of a cook. I'm glad Quinn picked a girl who knows her way around the kitchen."

A couple of hours later Ollie and Quinn stepped out into the moonlight and headed back across the yard toward his doublewide. She had put on a brave face for Mrs. Lewis, and again for Quinn, but today had shaken Ollie to her core. She knew most everyone in Red Creek, and everyone knew her. They also knew she had five brothers and a half-crazy daddy. She had always gone wherever she wanted and done whatever she pleased with no fear. After the town snubbed her, she hadn't felt scared, just angry and aggravated. Even at the construction site, dealing with the strange men from out of town, Eric had been there looking out for her.

Today, when Ed had pushed his disgusting belly against her, pinning her to the wall, breathing his stale cigarette breath into her face, she was petrified. She hadn't punched him in the face because she was brave. No, quite the opposite. The man had scared her to pieces.

"What's on your mind?" Quinn's deep voice cut through her thoughts, and she turned toward his shadowy form. He laid his hand on her shoulder, stopping her in the middle of the gravel road. "I'm sorry I snapped at you earlier. I've been thinking about why I was so grumpy. I guess I was worried about you."

Ollie's heart bumped in her chest as his hand pressed through her gauzy blouse, sending a wave of emotion through her body. She longed to reach up and stroke this man's jaw, rough with whiskers, but she squeezed her hand into a fist, pushing down her desire. She had run away from everything and everyone she loved so she could stand on her own, gain her freedom. Quinn Lewis was a steppingstone in her plan. If she touched him, gave in to this temptation, her steppingstone would turn into a stumbling block. "It's okay," she whispered through the darkness. "If I'm honest, I have to admit that I was a little scared today." Ollie stared through the moonlight into Quinn's face, his eyes reflecting the light. "I guess you were right about me working there."

"I'm sorry you had to go through that." Quinn's voice was soft and husky. He reached down and ran a finger along her cheek. "I should have been there for you."

"It turned out okay." Ollie took a step closer, her body wanting something. Her mind screamed she couldn't have. "I'm..."

Quinn leaned toward her, his lips pushing against Ollie's. Her arms reached up and curled around his neck, her fingers pulling him down, massaging his hairline. Something inside her exploded, and for a few brief seconds... an eternity, Ollie did not care about her vow to never get involved with a man again, to never be vulnerable again.

"Ollie."

"Yeah." Quinn pulled his lips away, and Ollie opened her eyes, her palm lingering on his neck, the warmth of his skin caressing her hand.

"Ollie." Quinn took another step back. "We'd better stop. Momma's probably watching us from the living room window."

"It's okay." Ollie grinned through the dim moonlight. "She probably can't see us in the darkness, and even if she can, we're married, remember?"

"True."

"No." Ollie pulled her arm from his neck as Quinn stepped closer. "I'm kidding." She placed her hand on his chest, ignoring the pounding of her heart. "You're right. I uh."

"I understand." Quinn stepped back. "You aren't over the food truck guy yet." He reached up and rubbed the back of his neck. "I understand." He started walking again, and Ollie followed. "Besides, I'm not really your type, and you're not mine."

"What makes you think you're not my type?" Ollie pushed down the annoyance in her voice. What was his type? *Probably women with big, bouncy... curls.*

"I figure you go for the guys with tattoos that are built a little more, well, solid."

"Solid?" Ollie's brow furrowed.

"Yeah, you know, like the food truck guy. The father of your baby."

"Eric?" Ollie bit her lip, stifling her chuckle. At least Quinn couldn't see the look on her face through the darkness. "I guess solid is one way to describe him. He's really a very nice man with a heart of gold. Once you get to know him, you forget about all the tattoos and his, well, his rotund appearance."

"If you say so." They stepped up to the porch, and Quinn stopped. "Can I ask you something, and you promise to tell me the truth?"

"Sure." Ollie leaned against the stair rail and looked at Quinn. The clouds that had been hiding the moonlight a few seconds before parted and her eyes met his. "I promise."

"Why did you get in my truck?" He looked down as Rambler ran up the stairs between them, then caught her gaze again. "You came to Floyd's trailer and found my truck on the day I was leaving, so you had obviously planned this thing out. Why me?"

"Oh." Ollie let out a sigh. "You might not like all the answers."

"That's alright. I want to know."

"It was three things. The first was that you were always polite and even-tempered. Even when some of the men were acting like jerks around you, you always kept your cool. You said nice things about your momma." Ollie tilted her head to the side. "That's why I figured I was really getting under your skin tonight when you were getting all uptight and grouchy. That's not like you."

"No." Quinn's eyebrows pulled together. "You're right. It's not. I'm surprised you know so much about me."

"I've been studying you ever since you came to work at the construction site."

"You've been planning this—whatever this is— for that long?"

"Yes." Ollie gnawed on her lower lip. "You want me to tell you the other reasons?"

Quinn studied Ollie's face. "Go ahead."

"I had narrowed down my ride options to three people, but when I heard you say you were leaving on that Friday, I moved you to the number one spot. Plus, you lived far enough away from Red Creek for me to make a clean start."

"Okay. So, you thought I would be a safe and quick ride and I lived in Louisiana. What's the last reason?"

"Promise not to get angry?" Ollie asked.

"I don't get angry, remember?"

"Well, with that scruffy beard and stringy long hair, I thought you were kind of—you know."

"No." Quinn stared at Ollie through the moonlight. "What?"

"I thought you were homely looking." Ollie shrugged her shoulders. "I figured I might be stuck in the truck with you for a while or even have to stay at your place for a day or two and..."

"And if you hitched a ride with an ugly guy, he would think

you were out of his league and not bother you," Quinn said, shaking his head. "Ollie Smith... Lewis, you are a piece of work."

"It sounds terrible when you say it like that, but I was getting in the truck with a strange man. I had to do everything I could to make sure I was safe."

"And what do you think now?"

"About what?" Ollie stared at Quinn, a strange glint in his eye.

"Are you safe from me? Am I out of your league?"

"I think it's getting late." Ollie hurried up the steps past Quinn and opened the front door. "Goodnight." She listened as Quinn's laughter floated in from the front porch. No, she was not safe, not after that kiss. She had to find a job quickly and get away from Quinn Lewis.

Chapter Ten

"Quinn, I made a decision today at church." Ollie dipped Quinn a plate of chicken pie and passed it across the bar to where he sat. It was odd how they had slipped into a routine on Sundays, every day, really. He told her he loved her chicken pie, so she had started making it for Sunday dinner, like they really were a normal married couple, coming home from church to eat lunch together and talk about the baby on the way. A month had passed since that night, the night of the kiss. She kept putting off telling him the truth, but today had to be the day. She couldn't keep doing this, lying to him like she was lying to everyone else in this town. He deserved better.

"I wanted to ask you about something the preacher said." Quinn pulled the plate in front of him and waited while she dipped hers, ignoring what she said. "He said that before a person gets saved, they are God's enemy. I don't get that. I'm not God's enemy. I don't consider myself to be anybody's enemy, really. Where is the preacher getting that from?"

Ollie slid onto the barstool and placed the steaming hot

plate of food in front of her. "He gets it from the Bible. I think it says it in Romans, but I'm not good at memorizing scripture, so I'm not sure. We'll have to Google it." She pulled a paper towel off the roll sitting on the bar and placed it in her lap. "It says something like while we were still his enemy, Jesus died for us."

"So, since I'm not saved, I'm God's enemy, but He's not mine?" Quinn pulled off his own paper towel and slowly placed it in his lap. "But how can I be His enemy if I don't even know Him? I don't get it."

"Because." Ollie pushed her lips together in a flat line. She was not a Bible scholar and definitely not equipped to tell the main person she was lying to every day how to get their life right with the Lord. "It's like this. When we sin, we are saying to God that His way is not good enough. That we understand better than the Creator of the universe what is right. Can you even imagine?"

"Kind of like a rat telling a person to get out of their house. Just because they live there, they assume they own the place."

"Nasty—but yeah." Ollie stirred the dumplings around on her plate. "God is perfect, and sin is—well—sin. We are all covered in the stuff. God wants us to be in His family, He wants us to know Him, but we can't because of the sin. He wanted me in His family so badly that He did the unthink-able." Ollie stared across the room, blinking back the tears that wanted to fall. "He gave Jesus to die in my place. The pain of sin was so... brutal. The Bible says Jesus felt like God had forsaken Him while He was dying." Ollie looked down at her fork, not meeting Quinn's gaze as he drank in her words. "My sins hurt me and the people around me, and I ache because I need to make things right." She pulled in a breath. "Jesus didn't hurt anybody, didn't sin against anybody, but my sins caused His death—and until I was saved, I didn't even care. Does that sound like a person who is God's friend?"

"My word." Quinn's eyes narrowed. "Yeah, I guess I am His enemy." He looked down at his food, lost in thought. He finally lifted his head. "But once you become a Christian, and you understand who God is and what He did for you, you go from being His enemy to His child. That's a lot to wrap your head around. I mean, bringing someone into your family who has done you so wrong for their entire life. I can't quite wrap my head around that."

Ollie's lips pushed up into a soft smile. "That's what makes God so amazing. He offered salvation to the very ones who hurt Him." Her eyes watered, and she picked the paper towel up from her lap. "Once a person truly sees who they are compared to God, I don't get how they can go on living until they get things right with Him."

"Ollie, I've done a lot of stuff in my life." Quinn pushed his plate away from the bar. "I've never killed anybody or anything like that, but there's a lot of things that nobody knows, even Drake. Are you sure God wants me? I mean, I don't have..." He paused, his voice catching in his throat. "I don't have anything to offer Him, and if someone hurt my son, even my nephew, the way I've hurt His, the last thing I could do was make that person a part of my family. Family is supposed to treat each other right."

"That's why God's love is better than our love. He loved us before we loved Him." Ollie reached over and squeezed Quinn's hand. "All you can offer God is yourself, who you are right now at this very moment. That's what He asks. Give Him yourself, and He will move in and straighten you up."

"How do I do that? Do I need to go back to the church and get the preacher?"

"No." A tear rolled down Ollie's cheek and splattered on her plate. "We can do that right now."

A couple of hours later, Ollie loaded the groceries from the cart into the backseat of Quinn's truck and climbed behind the wheel. It had been weird. That was the only way to describe the past month. Of course, she had not gone back to work for Ed. They had also stopped buying their gas there. She hadn't laid eyes on the man since the day she bloodied his nose, which was perfectly fine with her.

Quinn was right about jobs being scarce in Carson's Bayou. She had applied at the dollar store and the daycare at the Presbyterian church earlier in the week. Hopefully, now that people were getting to know her a little, one of these places would hire her. She'd put Esther's name down as a reference, so that should help. Having a sister-in-law as the nurse practitioner for the children's clinic certainly couldn't hurt. Ollie's eyes narrowed as she pulled into the street. The problem was, Esther wasn't really her sister-in-law because she and Quinn weren't really married.

That spot in the top of her stomach burned as the list of lies surrounding her life swirled through her head, squeezing in like a noose around her neck. She insisted on going to church every Sunday. Quinn was going with her. From the comments she caught from Drake, Esther, and the people at church, she had performed a small miracle by getting him there. Every Sunday, she would bow her head and tell the Lord that she was sorry for all the lies. Every Sunday, the Lord would push her to tell the truth, to come clean. Every Sunday, she would bawl her eyes out, silently telling God she was scared and didn't know how to do it.

Quinn would walk the aisle, making it public tonight at

church that he had given his life to the Lord. How could she possibly confess after what he said about family not hurting each other? She told him how Christians commit their lives to God, how He gives them the strength to live for Him and turn from the temptations of sin. How in the world could she tell him she wasn't pregnant?

It can't go on, though. I'm mocking God. I'm saying one thing and doing another, all while flouncing around here pretending to be someone I'm not. The burning in her stomach rose up her throat. Tears puddled in her eyes. She'd tell him tonight, after church. She had to. If he kicked her out, so be it. *I've got to do this. I can do this. God, I can only do this with your help.*

She pulled into the parking lot of the church where she had dropped Quinn off an hour before. After Quinn had prayed with Ollie and they had eaten lunch, which had grown cold before they got around to eating it, he had called the preacher and set up a meeting to talk. Ollie had dropped him at the church and used the time to do the grocery shopping, another habit they had fallen into over the past month.

Quinn had not attempted to kiss her again, but she caught him watching her, looking at her as she puttered around the house, and the looks made her catch her breath. Usually, when that happened, he would disappear for a while, go outside, or get in his truck and run some kind of errand, returning later like nothing was going on. *How? How in the world does that man think I could be attracted to Eric and not him?* Her smile melted into a somber gaze. *Because he thinks I'm having Eric's baby—duh.*

She watched Quinn step out of the church with the preacher at his side. Both men smiled as Quinn shook his hand. He headed back to the truck, and Ollie scooted over to the passenger's side. "It looks like everything went well."

"It did." Quinn slid behind the wheel and reached under the seat, adjusting it for his long legs. "I'm going to tell everyone about my decision tonight. He said that Drake has had them praying for me and Momma for years." He pulled the seatbelt across his middle and clicked it into place. "I told him that me and you aren't really married and about how you ended up here."

"You what?" Ollie's hand stopped midway across her lap, the seatbelt forgotten. "What did he say?"

"He said we needed to quit lying, but I guess we already knew that, huh?"

"Yeah." Ollie pulled the seat belt over and clicked it in place. "I guess so." She stared out the windshield. It was time to come clean. "So, we are going to let everyone know we're not married?"

"I think I have everything figured out." Quinn drove out of town and turned onto the gravel road that led to his house. "I'm gonna talk to Momma. You two have hit it off." Quinn looked over and smiled at Ollie. "That's no small task, either. Momma can be pretty opinionated when she wants to be."

"I kind of picked up on that."

"I'm going to explain to her why we lied in the first place, and why we can't keep on lying. She'll have a few words to say, I'm sure."

"I'm sure." Ollie rolled her eyes, not looking at Quinn. She liked his mother okay, but they weren't nearly as buddy buddy as Quinn thought. Unless she missed her guess, the woman could go from having your back, to stabbing you in the back in a New York minute, especially if she thought her son was getting taken advantage of.

"Don't worry." Quinn glanced over at Ollie. "I can handle Momma. She's got those two extra bedrooms. We will just move you into one of those."

Ollie bit her lower lip and frowned, still not looking at Quinn. "I'm not so sure about this."

"You can stay there at least until the baby comes, and you

get back on your feet. By then, we'll have figured out another plan." Quinn pulled into his driveway and looked at the red Chevy truck pulled in where he usually parked. "Who's that?"

Ollie's eyes stretched wide, and she looked from the truck to Quinn. "We have to talk, Quinn. I have something I need to tell you."

Eric stepped out of the truck and Quinn killed his engine. "Sure, Ollie, but we'd better take care of this first." He reached over and laid his hand on Ollie's shoulder. "Don't look so scared. I won't let him hurt you—or the baby."

Chapter Eleven

Quinn got out of his truck and walked over to where the burly man stood covered in tattoos, his bald head cleanly shaved. "Hey, Eric. How're you doing?" He stuck his hand out. "I see you tracked down Ollie."

"It took me a while." Eric shook Quinn's hand. "Is she okay?" He looked over Quinn's shoulder to the truck where Ollie still sat. "I need to talk to her."

"She's fine." Quinn pulled his hand back. "She's a little shook up about seeing you here—unannounced." He glanced at Ollie, watching him intently through the windshield. She sure was pale. "Look." Quinn turned to Eric. "Maybe you should just talk to me. I'm not sure she wants to see you right now."

"Really?" Eric's brow wrinkled. He looked from the truck to Quinn. "How much has she told you about..." He stopped and pushed his lips together. "No, man. I have to talk to Ollie."

The truck door slammed, and Quinn turned. Ollie walked

over to where they stood, a nervous smiled plastered on her face.

"Hey, Eric." Ollie wove her arm around Quinn's and leaned against him, pressing her head against his bicep. "I see you found me."

Quinn looked down at Ollie, closer to him than she had been since their kiss. *What's she up to?* "Let's go in the house and sit down. We all need to talk this out."

"Quinn, there's milk and meat in the backseat of the truck." Ollie looked up at Quinn, her voice a little too sweet. "Do you mind bringing it in, so it won't ruin?"

"Yeah." Quinn pulled his arm away from Ollie's. "Y'all wait right here."

"No. I'll take Eric on in and make us some coffee." Ollie blinked up at Quinn. "There's no need to stay out in this heat and melt."

She looked scared out of her mind a second ago, and now she's volunteering to take him inside? *What are you up to, Ollie?* "Okay." Quinn nodded at Eric. "I'll be right in." He watched Ollie smile nervously at the big man as they started up the front steps. *He doesn't know she's pregnant. Is she scared I'll tell him, or say something to give it away?* They disappeared inside the trailer, and Quinn hurried to his truck. He draped four plastic grocery bags on each arm and scooped up one more, holding it against his chest. He bumped the truck door shut with his hip and hurried up his front steps. For a brief second, he contemplated listening in on their conversation from outside the door, but the idea left his brain as soon as it formed. *If I want her to trust me, I have to act trustworthy.*

He slipped his hand down and opened the front door without dropping the gallon of milk nestled against his chest. The living room was empty. He crossed the room.

"If you won't go back with me, I've got to at least tell them where you are." Eric's deep voice echoed from the kitchen. "They've already talked to Jonah several times. I'm pretty sure your dad thinks the guy did something to you."

Quinn slowed his steps. Jonah? The man she left at the altar?

"I won't go back." Ollie's voice sounded as hard as stone.

"Everything okay in here?" Quinn stepped through the doorway, and Ollie, standing on the other side of the bar, turned away from him toward the coffeemaker.

Eric stepped over and took a couple of the bags from Quinn's arms. "Here. Let me help." He set the bags on the bar and waited while Quinn set down the rest of them. "I was telling Ollie that the town has been in an uproar since she left." He looked across the bar at Ollie, still not facing them. "Ollie has posters up all over town. It's only a matter of time before he finds you, too."

"Wait. Ollie?" Quinn raised his eyebrows.

"Ollie's brother, Oliver." Eric looked over at Quinn. "They both go by Ollie. It's a little crazy, but they're both called that about half the time."

"Ollie." Quinn walked around the bar and stood beside her. He laid his hand on her shoulder, and her muscles tensed under his fingers. "It's time we all three sat down and talked."

"Okay." Ollie turned and looked up at Quinn, her eyes hard with determination. She passed him two cups of coffee and picked up the third one. "I don't care what happens. I am not going back to Red Creek, Quinn. Neither one of you can make me."

"I'm not planning on trying to make you go anywhere you don't want to. I'm on your side, remember?"

"I hope you remember it after we're done talking."

Ollie followed the men to the living room and sat on the couch across from Eric, leaving plenty of room for Quinn on the other end. She gripped the warm mug in both hands, pulling up courage. How come she could be brave with her actions, but such a coward with her words?

"How did you figure out Ollie was with me?" Quinn asked.

"It wasn't easy." Eric leaned back on the love seat and set his coffee mug on the end table beside him. "When the Robinson men all showed up at my food truck looking for you," he nodded in Ollie's direction, "and then the police came asking questions a couple of days later. The workers got pretty tight-lipped."

"I didn't mean to cause a lot of trouble." Ollie looked up from her coffee mug. "With the way things have been since the..." She paused and looked at Quinn.

"I know you left some guy at the altar last year." Quinn met Ollie's gaze. "I texted Floyd the day you met Drake."

"You?" Ollie's eyes stretched wide. "You didn't say anything." She rubbed her lips together. "I should have told you, but I was scared you'd..." She looked over at Eric. *Why does telling the truth have to be so scary? But it wouldn't be if I didn't lie in the first place.*

"It's okay." Quinn's eyes met Ollie's, his soft smile similar to the one Drake had the day he found her in Quinn's kitchen. "It's water under the bridge. We can talk about all that later." He looked from Ollie to Eric. "You finally got somebody to tell you where Ollie had gone?"

"I didn't tell anybody where I was going," Ollie said, her eyes darting to Eric. "Not a soul. If I was going to tell anyone, it would have been..." She stopped and swallowed before the word you escaped her lips. Her eyes pulled from Eric to Quinn, staring at her, his face still calm. She leaned back on the couch and crossed her legs. Her knee bounced. *I've got to shut up or they're both going to turn on me.*

"Nobody told me where you went," Eric said. "But Floyd Pearson mentioned one day that you," he nodded toward Quinn, "left the same day Ollie disappeared. Nobody had really noticed. Men come and go from the site fairly often. That got me to thinking, though, and I started asking around to see who else had moved on the day you disappeared." He looked at Ollie and Quinn, both staring at him. "There was Quinn and one other man. I started with you." He looked at Quinn. "I had seen Ollie watching you a few times, so I followed my hunch."

"And you just drove over here after that?" Quinn asked.

"No. I talked to Floyd. I quizzed him, which wasn't hard. You know how Floyd talks."

"But Floyd didn't know anything to tell." Quinn's brow furrowed.

"No, but then I started knocking on the doors at his RV park. Floyd's neighbor saw Ollie climbing in your truck on the morning she disappeared."

"Who?" Ollie cut in. "I was so careful."

"Gary Phillips was the guy's name. He said he owed some back payments on his child support and didn't want to get involved with the law, so he hadn't said anything to anybody." Eric's eyes traveled down his muscular arms, covered in ink. "I tend to relate well with men trying to keep their heads low. After I figured out you hadn't been kidnapped or killed, I wasn't sure what to do." Eric tapped his fingers together. "Ollie, I'm your friend and only want what's best for you, but your family is going nuts."

"I can't go back, Eric." Ollie dropped her gaze to the coffee mug, forgotten in her hands. She felt the men's eyes boring into her. She lifted her head, her jaw firm. "There's a reason I left Jonah at the altar. A reason he wants to be kept a secret. Believe me, it's better that I stay away. Better for everyone involved."

"Your brothers are asking around." Eric said. "If I figured it out, they will too. Don't you think it would be better to at least let me tell your family where you are?"

"Ollie." Quinn reached over and laid his hand on her arm. "You don't have to be scared of this Jonah guy or your family." He looked over at Eric. "Or anybody else. I told you I'd keep you safe, and I will."

"Safe?" Eric's eyes narrowed. "Ollie, what's going on? You know your daddy or your brothers—or me—would chop off our right arms before we did anything to harm you."

Ollie's eyes darted from Quinn to Eric, both watching... staring... concerned. They had both helped her, stood by her when she needed them, and she'd lied to both of them. *Lord, give me courage.* She leaned forward and set her mug on the coffee table. "Quinn, he's right." She pulled in a slow breath. "I lied about needing to be protected. My family's a little crazy, and I guess I am too, but they wouldn't harm me."

Quinn eased his hand away. "And Eric?"

"I wouldn't hurt Ollie, man. She's like my little sister."

"Sister?" Quinn looked at Eric. "So, you're not—you've never been—involved?"

"You mean, have we hooked up?" Eric snorted. "No. Like I said, she's like my little sister."

"I um." Ollie swallowed. "I told Quinn that I'm pregnant."

"And that you're the father." Quinn's lips pushed into a flat line. He looked at Ollie. "So, if Eric isn't the father, then who is? Your old fiancé?"

"No." Ollie snapped at Quinn. "I'm not pregnant and I don't sleep around and shut your mouth before a fly crawls in. I didn't mean to lie to you, but you caught me off guard, and I blurted it out before I thought about it."

"You seem to do that a lot." Quinn grimaced. "A whole lot."

"I know," Ollie said. "I hate it about myself, so don't go lecturing me. Believe me, I lecture myself all the time." She looked over at Eric, watching them, mischief lighting his eyes. "What? Quit looking at me like that. This is serious."

"Of all the people in the world you could have picked to be your baby daddy, you picked me." Eric started to chuckle. "I guess I'm finding that a little funny." The chuckle grew louder. "I'm almost old enough to be your daddy. I think I may have even changed your diapers once or twice." He looked over at Quinn, frowning at both of them, and burst out laughing again.

Ollie grinned, but then looked at Quinn, fuming at both of them. She pushed her laughter down. "I'm really sorry, Quinn. I shouldn't have lied to you, but if you will just— forgive me?" Eric's laughter stopped, and the quiet was suddenly suffocating. "I don't deserve your forgiveness, I know. All I've done since you met me is use you." She looked at his face, emotions playing across his features as he replayed everything they'd been through over the past month. "If you want me to go, I'll go." She looked over at Eric. "But not with you, not back to Red Creek. That's the one thing I cannot do."

Quinn stood and walked over to the door.

"Where are you going?"

"I need some time to think." Quinn looked back at Ollie, hurt filling his eyes. "I don't know what I'm going to do. Eric —it was nice meeting you."

Chapter Twelve

Quinn pulled up in front of Drake's house and stared through the windshield. What happened to that feeling of peace and happiness that he had a few hours ago when he'd given his life to Christ?

Drake stepped onto the shady wrap-around front porch with a sweaty glass of ice tea in his hand. Quinn got out and walked to the steps. He hadn't consciously thought about going to Drake's, but this habit had formed before he was old enough to remember. Drake had been his sounding board to work things out such as when Momma caught him smoking one of her cigarette butts when he was five or when he got in trouble in grade school for punching out a bully or when he thought he'd gotten a girl pregnant in high school or when he'd gotten laid off last year from his job—his entire life.

"You alright?" Drake sat down on the steps of the porch and waited while Quinn sat beside him. "You want a glass of tea? There's some on the counter. Go fix yourself a glass."

"No. I'm good." Quinn looked over at the bird feeder hanging in the water oak shading the porch. A fat blue jay was hogging the food, running off any of the other birds that tried to eat. "How can someone say they're a Christian and then lie to you?"

"Ollie?" Drake took a sip of his tea and looked at his little brother's sagging posture and rounded shoulders. "You two have an argument? That happens to married folks, brother. You have to work through it and move on."

"Yeah—well—we're not married." Quinn stared across the yard. "She lied to you. I lied to you, too." The blue jay's screech, not a bird song like the other occupants of the tree, blared into the silence, warning the other birds to stay away from what belonged to him. Drake didn't answer, didn't gripe. *He knows me too well.*

Quinn smiled a sad smile. Drake could bark orders and become a drill sergeant so fast it would make your head spin, but Quinn would tell him what was on his mind if he waited. If he pushed into Quinn's personal affairs, Quinn would smile, or crack a joke, but he would walk away and take his burden with him. "I knew she was lying about some things in her past." Quinn reached down to the side of the steps and pulled up a single sprig of the perfectly green grass blanketing the front yard. "And when she told you we were married, I kept my mouth shut and let it ride, but today..."

"What was different about today? Sounds like you know she has a problem with the truth."

"I do, I mean." Quinn ripped the little blade of grass down the middle. "I thought we were growing closer. I thought." Quinn pulled in a deep breath of air and tossed the grass back into the yard. "I think I'm falling in love with her and I thought she was..."

"You thought because she might love you, she would be completely honest with you about everything?" Drake chuckled softly.

"Yeah—at least about the big stuff, the important stuff."

84

Quinn turned and looked at his brother. "Plus, she's a Christian. Shouldn't telling the truth carry a little more weight with her than it does with people who aren't?"

"Yes, it should, and I imagine it does." Drake's eyebrows pulled together. "Do you remember a while back when Gracie learned about smoking and tobacco in health? Remember how she had a fit about you dipping Skoal? How you promised her you'd quit?"

"Of course. She hounded me for a solid year, but I finally gave it up." He reached into his t-shirt pocket and pulled out a jolly rancher, sticky from the heat. "Now I'm addicted to these, but at least your daughter is happy."

"My point is this." Drake sat down, his tea glass between them. "She asked you to quit, and you said you would, but you kept dipping for months and months."

"Yeah, but quitting Skoal is hard. It wasn't like I didn't try."

"I know that. You tried every day, and every day you failed for a very long time. The whole time you were trying, Gracie was watching you like a hawk and reminding you of your promise, but she never quit loving you. She didn't understand how hard it was for you to quit. She thought you just didn't want to because you liked dipping, but she loved you through it."

"But lying isn't like dipping." Quinn peeled off the plastic from the sticky piece of candy. "All you do is—don't lie."

"Does she feel guilty for lying to you? Is she sorry about the lies?"

"Oh, yeah." Quinn nodded his head. "I watch her in church every Sunday. She cries her eyes out and prays silently pretty much throughout the entire service. I'm sure the lying is bothering her." He stuck the brown clear wrapper to his lips and licked off the green sugar goo. "She even told me that's why she acts that way every Sunday." The sweet sugar candy stuck to his teeth as Drake's words rolled around in his head. "I guess the part that hurts is that I thought she loved me enough, or at least respected me enough, to tell me the truth."

"The lying is not about you, Quinn. It's a weakness for her. Everyone has weaknesses, and the devil is an absolute expert at temping each of us until we act on our weakness. One of mine is my temper. I have to give it to the Lord all the time, or I would still be lashing out and cracking skulls."

"So, I just forgive her, act like everything is honky dory?"

"Forgive her, yes, but you help her see that she can over-come this. Remind her she can trust you with the truth. Hold her accountable, but with love." He reached over and slapped his little brother on the shoulder. "Always with love. That's the difference between helping her and nagging her. But the truth is, she's got to give the problem to the Lord and trust Him to help her. We become instruments God uses to help her overcome the sin—or we become the tools the devil uses to help her stay trapped in the sin."

"That's kind of deep."

"Not really." Drake stood up. "Everybody plays for one team or the other, little brother. Most of us just don't believe it or choose to ignore it." He reached down and picked up his tea glass. "I've got to go get ready for church tonight. You want to come in? The kids are with Esther at her grandma's, but you can hang out until I have to leave."

"No. I've got to get home. I've got to get ready for church tonight, too."

"I'm glad you're coming." Drake frowned. "If you aren't married, and you are living together... are you?"

"Shacking up? No, but I got saved this afternoon, and I'm not going to start off lying. Either she will have to move out or I will."

"Wait. You got saved?"

Ollie watched Eric's truck pull out of the driveway heading back to Red Creek. She looked down at the money in her hand and sighed. The only way he had agreed to leave was if she bought a phone and agreed to text him her new number. She had her old phone, but refused to get it turned back on. All her family and half of Red Creek had her old number.

"If I don't hear from you by tomorrow night, I'll be driving right back over here," he said, shoving the two hundred dollars into her fist. "Don't tell yourself I won't because you know I will. Get one of those pre-paid phones, and send me your number. I won't tell your people where you are, but I need to hear from you."

"Okay, but I'll pay you back."

"Whatever." Eric had kissed her on the top of the head, like her dad would do when he was having a rare moment of tenderness. "You're making a mistake, though. Them brothers of yours will not stop until they find you. And Ollie is going nuts."

"I'll—figure something out."

But what? With the money Eric gave her, she now had a grand total of nine hundred dollars. If she had a car, she could leave and stretch the money until she figured things out. Sleeping in a car wouldn't be that bad. Quinn's eyes, filled with hurt when he walked out earlier, played across her brain. *Lord, I'm so sorry. How do I stop hurting people with my mouth? I'm such a coward.*

She turned to walk inside, but stopped as Quinn's truck turned into the yard. She watched him get out of the truck, not mad or upset, at least not that she could tell. She had studied him for months from the food truck, and then over the past few weeks, she had really gotten to know him. He liked old-school country music, black t-shirts, and blue jeans. He kept candy stashed in his truck to nibble on. He loved his family more than anything and would do anything for them. He liked westerns and grew up watching Bonanza reruns. He pretended he was Little Joe as a kid. He was good and honest and kind and didn't lose his temper... *and I've fallen in love with him.*

It was true. She could lie to everybody else, but not to herself, at least not about this. He shut his truck door and leaned down and petted Rambler. Her heart squeezed. *What do I do? What if he doesn't love me? He kissed me, though. But just that once. But he's a gentleman. What does it matter? I've betrayed him, and he knows I'm a liar.*

"I'm glad you're still here." Quinn climbed the porch steps. "Where's Eric?"

"He's gone back to Red Creek." She shoved the two one-hundred-dollar bills into her jeans pocket. "I didn't have anywhere to..." The words died on her lips. *I don't want his pity.* "I'm figuring things out. If you'll let me stay tonight, I'll be ready to leave by in the morning." *I don't know how, but that's not his problem.*

"I want you to keep staying here."

Quinn stepped closer, and Ollie's eyes squeezed shut as her nose pulled in his scent. It would be so easy to forget what she wanted, forget what she had left behind, and what was following her and would probably be on her doorsteps soon. To spend the next few days or weeks or months, however long it took for her past to catch up with her, to drag her down. To take him down with her. No. If she truly cared for him, she wouldn't do that, and she cared for him.

"But." She stepped to the side as he eased past her, his

arm brushing against hers. He continued to the front door, and she reached up, placing her hand on his back. "Quinn?" He stopped, but her hand lingered, longing for more.

"Yeah?" He didn't turn around.

"Um." She stepped closer. Would it be so wrong to stay here? To be near him? Her hand eased up his back to his shoulder as she drew closer, her heart racing in her chest. "Are you sure us living together is... impossible?" She felt his muscles tighten under her touch, and he pulled away. "I'm sorry." She dropped her hand, her cheeks flaming red. "I didn't mean..."

"I'm moving in with Momma when we get back from church tonight." He stepped through the door into the cool air-conditioned living room, his back still to Ollie. "I've got to get ready. I'm walking that aisle. I'd like for you to come, but if you don't, that's okay."

Ollie watched him disappear through the living room and listened as his bedroom door closed. How? How could he come to know the Lord today and already have more strength and wisdom and—everything than her? *What's wrong with me, God? Why am I so broken?* Tears dripped down Ollie's face. She stumbled to her bedroom and fell onto the bed. Exhaustion weighed her down, and she closed her eyes, sobs wetting her pillow.

You can't serve two masters. The memory verse floated into her head, but she was too tired. What was the rest of it? She would look it up later. Right now, she needed to grab a nap before they went to church. She listened as the shower turned on in the other room. *What can wash away my sins...* The tune she'd known since before she could remember drifted through her mind as sleep took her away.

Chapter Thirteen

Two weeks later, Ollie opened the refrigerator and pulled out the milk. She wasn't hungry. She wasn't anything, really, just going through the motions. Quinn had been true to his word and told everyone that their marriage was fake. It was pretty amazing. He had stood at the front of the church, said he had given his life to Christ, then taken full responsibility for her entire fiasco.

"Ollie rode back with me from Alabama because of some difficulties she was having. She didn't have a place to stay." He'd looked across the congregation without any signs of fear or worry. "She stayed with me. She was scared of what everyone would think and told my brother we were married. Don't blame her for this. I shouldn't have put her in that position. She was in a strange town with no one to help her and did the best she could. Other than the lie, she has nothing to be ashamed of. After tonight; however, I'm moving in with my momma." His eyes scanned the room, then stopped on her face in the back. "I'm telling all of you this tonight because, according to what I'm learning about my new faith, you all are my family now. Family looks out for each other, and I know y'all are going to want to help me and her do what is right."

She had held her breath, not sure what the people of the church would think of Quinn with his abrupt disclosure of their recent sin right after giving his life to the Lord. First one person, a little man on a walker with fuzzy gray hair, sitting in the second row, had slipped into the aisle. He'd embraced Quinn in a hug and squeezed in between him and the preacher. After that, it was like a floodgate opened as the rest of the church moved forward to welcome Quinn into the church as a family member.

"Come on, Ollie." Esther, her pretend sister-in-law, had stepped across the aisle. "Let's go let Quinn know we love him." Tears filled Ollie's eyes that evening, and she had been fighting them away ever since.

She had not heard from the Presbyterian church's daycare about that job, and the dollar store hired someone else. One of the ladies at the church said the school was needing another janitor, but not until the end of the summer. Ollie poured the milk over her bowl of Lucky Charms and padded to the living room, her feet bare. She had thanked the lady, but she was not going to be in Carson's Bayou that long.

Quinn stopped by every evening when he got off work to see if she needed anything. He'd get his mail from the box and chat a few minutes, then go across the road. He picked her up for church, took her to the store, did anything she asked him to in his polite way, but whatever had been growing between them had been broken by her lies.

Last night after church, he had been more like his old self. "I wish you could have seen Momma. She was so mad she couldn't even talk, which happens about once every twenty years."

Ollie had looked over at Quinn and smiled, drinking in his carefree tone. "Poochie smelled bad?"

"Awful." Quinn's eyes twinkled with laughter. "I don't know where she found a skunk, but she got sprayed good. Then she came right on in the house through her little door and climbed right up in bed with Momma like she was wearing some expensive perfume."

"Poor Mrs. Lewis."

"Poor Poochie." Quinn pulled his truck up in front of his trailer. "I told Momma she didn't need to put that dog door in back when she moved into the house, but she said Poochie was her baby and needed to be able to get inside when she needed in." He put the truck in park and looked over at Ollie, grinning. "Her baby got a midnight scrub with the water hose and Tide. Now she looks like a giant rat. Momma shaved her from one end to the other, even her little nubby tail."

"Aww." Ollie picked her Bible up from the seat between them. "Does she smell better?"

"Yeah. Momma burned the dog hair this morning in the metal barrel out back."

"Is that what the horrible odor was?" Ollie wrinkled her nose. "I don't see how your momma could stand to keep the fire going. It burned my eyes way over here."

"Momma is as tough as nails." His eyes softened, and he looked at Ollie. "Kind of like you."

Heat crept up Ollie's neck, but pleasure filled her heart. "You think I'm tough?"

"You climbed in my truck without knowing me from Adam. You punched the town creep in the face, you moved to a strange town and fell right in, making a go of things. Yeah, I'd say you're pretty tough."

"I don't feel tough." Ollie tucked her hair behind her ear. "I just—survive." She bit her lower lip. "Do you want to come in? For some coffee?"

Quinn had stared at her for a long time. "Ollie, I don't know what all has gone on with you, and I don't expect you to tell me. Until you can trust me enough to be honest with me about whatever it is you are running from, I'd better keep my distance." He stared at her face. "I can't allow myself to get too close to you. It's too hard."

"It's okay." Ollie looked down, blinking back the emotions that wanted to carry her away. "I shouldn't have asked." She pulled the latch and opened the truck door. "Tell your mother hello."

This morning she let the tears fall, splattering into her milk. Last night it became plain that whatever she was waiting for, whatever she thought was going to happen in this weird scenario, was not going to happen. If she didn't make a change, she would sit over here day in and day out feeling sorry for herself, mooching off Quinn's soft heart, while she pined away for some other life. It was time to move on, car or no car, money or no money. She'd land on her feet, just not in Carson's Bayou, not with Quinn Lewis.

She stirred her spoon around in her milk. Didn't she want freedom? Didn't she want to make her own rules, not have to worry about anybody else or how her actions would affect them? She rubbed her hands across her cheeks, swiping away the last of the tears. She could call her momma in Nashville. Why not? Her mother had written to her on her birthday back when she was thirteen, telling her to come visit when she got old enough. Well, she was old enough—and desperate enough to look her up. It was time to move on. Quinn's smile spilled into her mind. *He's better off without me.*

"I thought you had more sense than that." Mrs. Lewis stared at Quinn across the dining room table. "I admit she fooled me for a hot minute too, but son, open your eyes. She's using you."

"Momma, she didn't ask me to move over here. I offered."

"And that just makes you a bigger idiot." Mrs. Lewis jabbed her fork into the piece of biscuit on her plate and mopped it around in the red gravy. "You pay the light bill, you buy her groceries, you cart her around wherever she wants to go. If that's not a freeloader, then I don't know what is."

"She's down on her luck." Quinn shoved a piece of biscuit into his mouth. "You've been down on your luck before. What about when Dad died? Wouldn't it have been nice to have gotten a little help from somebody until you got back on your feet?"

"Son, if there's one thing I know for certain in this life, it's that the only help you'll ever really get is from your own right arm. When I buried your daddy, I went to work doing whatever I could to feed and clothe you three boys. I didn't sit around and wait for some starry-eyed sugar daddy to come along and put me up."

Quinn shoved his chair back from the table and stood up. "She's not like that."

"If it quacks like a duck." Mrs. Lewis watched Quinn walk out of the kitchen. "Where are you going?"

"Out."

Quinn pulled his keys from his jeans pocket and slid behind the seat of his truck. *Where am I going?* He looked across the gravel road to his trailer. Last night, when Ollie invited him in, the urge to pull her across the seat, to take her in his arms had been so strong, almost too strong. Was she using him? She had used him before. *God, help me be strong.*

He shoved the key in the ignition and pulled onto the road. A light shined from the trailer, his bedroom light. What was she doing in there? There wasn't anything in there he minded her seeing. He'd brought his laptop over when he'd moved in with his momma, and he locked all his important papers up in a metal box in the bottom of his gun safe. Not that it mattered. Ollie had a good heart. She had fallen on hard times, but she had a good heart.

He gave the truck some gas and headed into Carson's Bayou. He'd find something to do until Momma went to bed. He'd been there two weeks, and her opinion of Ollie and their situation was becoming more and more sour... and more and more vocal. It was bad enough when she found out he'd become a Christian.

"So, you up and joined the Bible thumpers?"

"You should come to church with me sometimes, Momma. You would probably like it."

"No, thank you." Mrs. Lewis had pulled a long drag from her cigarette, an intimidation technique she mastered from years of practice. "Me and God have an understanding. I take care of myself down here and don't bother Him, and He takes care of things up there and doesn't bother me."

He'd tried a couple of more times. He really tried, just like Drake tried to explain to his mother about Jesus and her need for Him, but until she wanted to listen, he might as well have been talking to Poochie.

He drove into town and pulled into the Gumbo Hut. The couple of bites of biscuit had not filled him up. He ordered a catfish po'boy and pulled out his phone while he waited for his meal to arrive. He scrolled down to Floyd's number. Who was Jonah Blue? The name of the man that owned the hotel he'd been working on was Blue.

The waitress arrived with his meal, and he laid his phone down beside his plate. He needed to let that go. If Ollie wanted him to know what happened, she would tell him. Maybe if he knew about what occurred, he could understand her better. Maybe he could figure out a way to get her to open up to him if he understood what happened. He put down his po'boy and wiped his greasy fingers on a paper napkin.

He picked up his phone and punched in the text.

> Tell me about Jonah Blue.

He sipped his Coke, waiting for Floyd to respond. Floyd loved to gossip better than any woman. If he didn't answer, his phone was dead, or he was.

> He's the only son of Gordon Blue, the guy building the hotel. The old man owns practically every piece of property worth owning in Red Creek. His son works for him. I've never met the kid, but the old man is a good guy. Why? What's up?

Were Ollie's people wealthy? When she broke it off with Jonah Blue, had they shunned her to working in a food truck?

> What about the Robinsons? Are they wealthy too?

Quinn figured all along that Smith wasn't Ollie's real last name. Robinson was what Eric called her family.

Three laughing emojis popped onto the screen.

> Are you kidding? The old man has a place he calls an antiques and collectables store, but it's just a junk yard. Why are you asking? Have you found sausage girl?

Chapter Fourteen

Ollie put her note on the fridge between a picture of Quinn's nieces and nephew, Molly, Gracie, and Scout, and a snapshot of Quinn and Rambler that looked at least five years old. She pealed up a rubbery state of Arkansas magnet and secured her letter. He had to see it when he came in. He always grabbed a couple of jolly ranchers from the fridge before he did anything else.

She walked into the living room, looking around the spotless house, so different from what she had stepped into the day she arrived. She swallowed the lump in her throat. It was for his good and hers, too. He deserved an honest woman who could give him a good life. *You could do that*. She pushed down the thought along with the guilt of slinking away without saying goodbye.

She picked up her backpack from the couch. What would Quinn or Eric or Daddy say if they found out she was hitch-hiking? She sighed and hoisted everything she owned onto her back. Time to be brave again.

Tires crunching through gravel sounded out front, and a truck slowed in front of the trailer. He couldn't be getting home early today. He never came home early. If he saw her leaving, he'd want to talk about everything, help her, stay involved. *Sneak out the back and wait for him to read the note.* That would work. He'd leave after reading her letter, then she could get away. She started toward the laundry room.

Knock, knock, knock. Quinn didn't knock. She turned and eased back across the living room, careful to keep her steps silent. She peaked through the curtains. Oliver! Tears filled her eyes, and she jerked open the front door, forgetting she had abandoned him, that he might be furious with her. She threw her arms around her twin, pressing her head against his chest. "You found me."

"You didn't make it easy." Oliver's large hands stroked his sister's back. He held her there for a few seconds, then pushed her away. "You've got to come home with me."

Ollie's smile froze. She slipped her backpack from her shoulders and stared at her brother. "You know how things are for me back there. I can't go back."

"Ollie, Dad's in jail."

"What?" Ollie's jaw dropped. "What happened?"

"He drove over to Jonah's house with his shotgun and threatened to blow him away if he didn't tell him what he'd done with you."

"No, no, no!" Ollie pushed back from her brother and ran her fingers through the top of her blond hair. "Has he lost his ever-loving mind?"

"What did you think was going to happen?" Oliver's eyes narrowed. "You disappeared off the face of the earth without so much as a see you later. You know how Daddy is about you." His voice softened. "The sheriff had to get the doctor over to the jail yesterday. He was having chest pains."

Color drained from Ollie's face. "Is he okay?"

"They took him to the ER and checked him out. The doctor said it's stress."

"Where is he now?" If something happened to her daddy because of all of her mess, how would she cope?

"Back in jail." Oliver rolled his eyes. "The sheriff told him he'd let him go home if he promised to leave Jonah alone, but Daddy wouldn't have that. He said he would be back at the guy's house before the sheriff got back to his office."

Ollie huffed out a breath of air. "Of course he did." She reached down and stroked Rambler's head. "Can't you just tell him you found me, and that Jonah had nothing to do with me leaving?"

"No, because we both know that's a boldface lie."

"Well." Ollie looked down at the dog, not meeting her brother's pointed stare. "Jonah didn't directly have anything to do with me leaving." Her eyebrows drew together. "Are you sure you can't fix this? You know what a stir this is going to cause if I go back."

"Don't you think that I would have done fixed this if I could have?" Oliver shook his head. "You have to tell me what Jonah's holding over your head. Until you tell me, there's not much I can do."

"I..." Ollie tilted her head up and looked at her brother, his features so similar to hers, but his skin sun kissed from being outside. "I can't tell you." Her shoulders slumped as she stared past Oliver to Mrs. Lewis's house across the road. Was she watching them now? Probably.

If she went back today, would she ever get the courage to strike out on her own again? If she didn't go back, could she live with herself if something happened to her daddy? "Okay." She straightened up. "I'll go back, but you have to promise me something."

"What?" Oliver reached down and picked up Ollie's backpack.

"You won't ask me any questions about—this." She jerked

her head toward the trailer behind her. "I don't want any questions about Carson's Bayou."

"What did he look like?" Quinn raked his hand across his jawline as he listened to his momma. "Was it the same guy that was here before?"

"No." Mrs. Lewis dropped her cigarette on her front porch and rubbed it into the wooden floor with the toe of her house shoe. "This man was younger and easy on the eye." She squatted down and retrieved the demolished butt. "And she was all over him, wrapping her arms around him right there on your front porch for everybody to see."

"Who's gonna see, Momma? Besides you?"

"That's not the point and you know it."

"The point is, that this is none of your business." Quinn felt in his pocket for a jolly rancher, but he was out. "I'm sure Ollie had a reason for leaving." He stepped off the porch. "Don't hold supper for me."

"Where are you going?" Mrs. Lewis put her hands on her hips. "Can't you see that girl was just using you?"

"Home, Momma." Quinn turned back and looked at his mother. "If you have to know, I'm going back to my house, taking a shower, and getting into my bed. Do you have a problem with that?"

"No." Mrs. Lewis reached out and laid her hand on Quinn's shoulder. "I'm sorry she hurt you, son. She had me fooled for a while, too."

"Bye, Momma." Quinn stepped away, not looking back at his mother. The sky in front of him was a mixture of pink and orange with the setting sun. The katydids sang their usual evening tune as he trudged across the road and up his porch steps. Rambler crawled from under the trailer and stretched. "Come on, boy." Quinn slapped his leg, and the dog trotted up the steps to his side. "Might as well come on in. This house is too big for me to be in here all by myself."

He unlocked the front door, and the dog walked in ahead of him. He turned on the lights. The coolness of the air-conditioned house felt good after being in the heat all day. Rambler hopped up in his old spot on the love seat. Quinn's eyes roamed around the room, spotless, just like it had been ever since Ollie moved in. He dropped his keys on the coffee table. Would she be back? *No. She won't.* He wasn't sure how he knew she was gone for good, but he knew.

He walked into the kitchen and flipped on the light. No signs of Ollie there either—except... his work boots echoed on the floor as he hurried over to the fridge and jerked down the note.

> Quinn,
>
> First of all, thank you for everything you have done for me. You took me in and treated me so well, even after the way I treated you. You amaze me. You've only been saved for a very short time, but you act more like Christ than a lot of other people I grew up in church with. And, well, you act more Christ-like than me, too. I'm sorry about all the lies. I never mean to tell them. They just happen, then I get scared, and you know what happens.
>
> I decided last night after talking to you that

it's time for me to move on. I can't keep living in your house forever. I've got to get a job and build my own life, and you've got to take your life back. I've decided to go to Nashville and stay with my mother for a while.

You were right about keeping your distance from me. It's better for both of us if we go our separate ways. Pray for me. Forgive me.

Ollie

Nashville? Who had she called to pick her up and take her to Nashville? *She might be lying again.* What now? He opened the refrigerator and scooped up a couple of pieces of candy. He grabbed the half empty milk jug and closed the door. He wouldn't go after her. That would be a stupid move. He unscrewed the lid and tilted the jug back against his lips, taking a long drink. *What would she do if I caught up with her? She's made it perfectly clear that she's done with me.*

He set the jug on the counter and tossed the little red lid in the sink. But who was that guy? It couldn't be her old fiancé, not after she ran out on him on their wedding day. *Why not? You're standing here thinking about running after her? Maybe this guy has it bad for her, too.*

Quinn unwrapped a jolly rancher as he walked into the living room. He turned off the light and watched the moonlight flood through the windows. Rambler lifted his head and looked at Quinn, waiting to see if he would be ushered outside like he had been for the past several weeks. "Go back to sleep, boy." Quinn patted his dog's head as he walked by. "You think she's okay?" He scratched the dog's neck. Rambler's droopy eyes stared up at Quinn, glinting in the darkness. "Yeah, you're right. She can take care of herself."

Quinn stepped into the hall and started toward his bedroom, but turned. He walked into her room and looked around. A hairband lay on the bedside table, but he could find nothing else of hers. He sat on the bed. "God, I don't understand why she came into my life and then left again. Was it to get me to you? If that's the reason, then I'm grateful—but Lord, this is—hard." He listened, half expecting to hear the front door open, to hear Ollie call his name, but everything was silent. "Watch over her, God, please."

He picked up the pillow where she had slept every night since she moved in and shoved his face down into the soft feathers. Honeysuckle filled his nostrils, just like it had that night they had kissed. He eased over onto the bed and stretched out, not bothering to take off his work boots. Where was she now? Was she safe? She had reached out to him last night, and he'd pushed her away. Now she was gone.

She'd been gone several hours by the time he'd gotten home. Momma hadn't called him to tell him about her leaving. She'd waited until he drove up, then met him on her front porch, ranting about what she'd seen. Had she waited on purpose so he wouldn't go look for Ollie? Probably. Momma was nervous, suspicious, overprotective... all of that, but she wasn't dumb. She could play dumb when she wanted to, and if he'd asked her why she didn't call him as soon as Ollie left, she would have done that.

No. Momma wanted Ollie out of his life, and now she was gone. It wasn't Momma's fault. It was his. He closed his eyes and breathed in the fragrance of her body spray. It wasn't meant to be. He would go back to his bachelor life like before. He'd forget about Ollie Robinson. Not forget, never forget, but he'd learn to move on without her. Somehow.

Chapter Fifteen

Fighting. That was the best way to describe what was going on inside her. They pulled down the narrow gravel drive, complete with potholes that would knock your vehicle out of line if you didn't know how to strategically dodge them. Ori, the wild child, actually blew a tire one time back when he was a teen, racing to get home before their daddy woke up and discovered he was out all hours of the night.

Redbud, persimmon, and magnolia trees mixed in with the oaks and pines shading both sides of the drive. Daddy loved living down this secluded path. "You can love your neighbor a lot easier when there's a good stretch of trees between them and you," he'd often told her through the years when she would complain about being away from her school friends all summer. "City life is for city folks."

A soft smile crept across Ollie's face. City life. Dad called living in Red Creek city life. When she was older and worked at her dad's junk store after school, in typical teenage style, she longed to be home... out of the "city." Their store was not a posh antique or thrift store like the ones on those Hallmark movies or reality shows. Nope. It was more like Fred Sanford moved down south and taught her dad how to set up a business. During her teen years, it was hard to act like she didn't care when her peers came in and made fun of her dad and his store, but she'd done it. She'd been acting—pretending for so long that it became second nature.

The truck rumbled through the opening of the rusty metal fence surrounding the yard. The gate had been missing since before she was born. Their great grandfather built the old house over a century ago, and now it was practically falling down around their ears. It sounded romantic in her head, but in reality, it was a drafty old house with chilly rooms, peeling paint, rotting floorboards, and a rusty tin roof. Something was always... always broken.

Still, she had missed the place. In the spring and early summer, the enormous azalea bushes grew along the edge of the fence in the back, the wisteria dripped from the oak trees looking like clusters of grapes and smelling like heaven, and the wild iris and the daffodils took over the ground out by the rusted-out swing set. They all gave the place, run down and wild as it was, a sense of beauty. Even if nobody else cared about the old home place anymore, God did.

She opened the truck and jumped over the bathtub sized mud puddle at her feet. The rooster, her rooster, perched on the narrow rusty fence pole, along with the few hens that loved to do their business on the front porch and lay their eggs under the house. She counted the shadowy sleeping figures through the dark starlight. Seven, good. A fox or a stray dog hadn't killed any while she was away.

"Doesn't look like anything has changed while I was gone." Ollie looked around the front yard, dusty and littered with "merchandise" daddy had either rejected for the store or hadn't gotten around to hauling into town yet. She headed to the front porch, her feet knowing where to walk and dodge obstacles strewn over the ground from years and years of practice.

"Not out here." Oliver followed her up the front porch steps, missing the second step that wouldn't hold a grown man's weight if he didn't know where to put his foot. "But everything else has."

He reached in front of her and opened the door—the unlocked door. They walked in and Ollie looked around while Oliver found the light switch, not near the front door, but over on the wall leading to the bathroom. The family had added electricity and indoor plumbing to the home as they came available and as the Robinson clan could afford them. The work was headed up by whoever in the family at the time claimed to know how to plumb or do electrical work, with the rest of the clan helping and throwing in their two cents worth of knowledge. Light switches were in awkward places, bathrooms were stuck in unusual areas, hot water faucets often gave cold water and vice versa, and the refrigerator was in the corner of Ori's bedroom.

The mystery behind that reasoning had finally come to light when Ollie was in third grade and spent the night with a friend. Until then, it hadn't dawned on her how odd their house was. "Daddy, why is our refrigerator in Ori's room? It's in the kitchen in Becca's house and at Aunt Sadie's house, too."

"Stretch your arms out as wide as you can." Daddy watched Ollie do as she was told. "Now go walk into the kitchen." Daddy continued peeling his apple and throwing the pieces of peel off the porch to the chickens. Ollie disappeared inside the house, the screen door slamming behind her. "Don't put your arms down," he called, waiting for her to return.

Ollie reappeared beside him a few seconds later, the

screen slamming behind her again. "I can't. I don't fit through the door."

"Neither does the refrigerator. Your momma bought that big ole thing way back when you were a baby. We barely got the other one out, but that double wide contraption wouldn't go in. I told her we'd put it in the other room for a couple of days until I could fix the door." He sliced off a bite of the apple and passed it to Ollie. "I never got around to it, then she left, and I didn't see the point in moving it."

Sometimes Ollie wondered why her mother left, sometimes she didn't. Ollie looked around the living room, cluttered with books and magazines, the ancient high back piano on the far wall, guitars propped on either side. "Let me put my backpack in my room and splash a little water on my face, and I'll be ready."

She went down the dark hall, not bothering to turn on the light. Soft snoring came from Owen and Ori's room across the hall from hers. Odi and Oscar had moved out when they came back from college, but the rest of Daddy's birds were slow in leaving the nest. Ollie stepped into her bedroom. The white paint peeling from the shiplap boards, the ancient white bedspread with the little knots tied all over it, the paper thin curtains with faded pink roses, the letter 'O' on the wall behind her bed where she had picked the paint off the wall the week she had chicken pox and had to stay in her room. All the same. She dropped the backpack on the bed. This was her life. No need to cry or complain. The prodigal had returned.

Quinn looked across the table at Mr. Randall, the mentor assigned to him by the pastor after he walked the aisle. After he read Ollie's note, he had called him and asked if he could come for their session a day early. Mr. Randall, a widower in his early seventies, had agreed immediately, and now they sat at the kitchen table, each with a glass of tea.

The old man met with him twice a week to talk, pray, and answer any questions he had about his Bible reading. That's how it had started anyway. Mr. Randall had suggested Quinn read through the book of John. Now Quinn had read through the book four times. The old man had become more than a teacher of the Bible for Quinn, quickly morphing into a sort of father figure.

"She was gone when I got home this evening. She left me a note thanking me for helping her. She said she was going to her momma's in Nashville."

"You sound surprised."

Quinn's eyebrows pulled low. "Well, yeah. I am." He looked down at the Bible, open to the passage where Jesus raised Lazarus from the dead. "I mean, I just assumed she was planning on staying around."

"Did you give her a reason to stay around?" Mr. Randall sipped his iced tea. "You told me before you were developing feelings for Ollie. Did you tell her this?"

"Sort of." Quinn thought about their last conversation, the things he said. "Actually, I sort of told her I couldn't trust her and that I was going to keep my distance."

"I see." Mr. Randall set the tea glass down and pushed his lips together. "Do you know what I find so amazing about Jesus and His time here on earth?"

Quinn blinked. *I guess we are done talking about Ollie.* "I'm impressed by how He stayed so laser focused with everything He went through and never gave up. He never forgot what He was here to do."

"Yes, that's very impressive, isn't it?"

"Yes, sir."

"Have you thought about how He never gave up on His friends?"

"What do you mean?" Quinn leaned back in the metal chair that looked like it had been around since the seventies. "The disciples?"

"Yes, and Mary and Martha, and others, but mainly the disciples." His lips pushed up in a soft smile. "Can you imagine going on a three and a half year camping trip with twelve of your closest friends? Hanging out with them day and night, explaining to them over and over why you were there. Showing them what you could do and why you were doing it. Then, after days and weeks and months of patiently working with them, bringing them along, they still don't understand you. Even talk down to you—even betray you?"

Quinn stared. Different stories from the book of John played through his head as Mr. Randall's words soaked in.

"Even with all their pettiness and grumbling and just not getting what Jesus was all about, the Messiah stayed right there with them. He didn't cut them from the group, tell them He needed to keep His distance because they weren't good enough." Mr. Randal chuckled. "I can't even imagine the frustration that would cause." He looked Quinn in the eye. "Or the heartache. But He loved them anyway. He loved them enough to be honest and truthful, even when they weren't, and to stand by them even when they didn't stand by Him."

"I'm an idiot." Quinn sat forward and pushed his fingers through his hair. "Here I am a Christian all of five seconds, and I decide to push Ollie away because she doesn't open up to me."

"I think you are protecting yourself." Mr. Randall picked up his tea glass and drained the last swallow. "She is getting too close to you, and since she's not what you expected her to be..."

"You can say that again."

"I think she scares you a little." Mr. Randall stood up and stepped over to the counter, refilling his glass. "I've watched you around her. There's something there between you two, and I think this scares you."

Quinn rolled over and picked up his cell phone. Four a.m. He nudged his leg over, and Rambler grunted. It had taken the dog all of three hours before he found his way into the bedroom to sleep. Quinn didn't blame the animal. Everybody needed somebody. Rambler needed him, and he needed Ollie. Even in the short time they'd known each other, he'd already started taking for granted that she would be there when he got ready to take the next step... waiting for him to decide that she was good enough. *Idiot.*

He rolled over and put his feet down, his toes touching the cool wooden floor. No need to try to sleep. Everything Mr. Randall said from earlier that evening kept playing over and over in his head. She needed a true friend. She'd reached out to him, and he'd pushed her away. Mr. Randall was right. Time to be honest with himself, expect the same thing from his own heart that he was demanding from hers. He was already in love with her. He already missed her. He already couldn't sleep, wondering where she was and who the guy was that she had left with.

He plodded to the kitchen and fixed a cup of coffee. He could leave in an hour if he hurried. Nashville was a big town, but once he found out her mother's name from Eric, he could track her down. Then what? He wasn't sure, but he couldn't leave things like they were. He needed to let her know he had feelings for her. If she didn't return those feelings...

He sipped the steaming black coffee, letting it burn a path down his throat. Would her not loving him mean he would stop loving her? Mr. Randall's voice played in his head. *But He loved them anyway.* Quinn stood. He would find her, explain why he had pushed her away, explain why he had followed her. That was all he could handle thinking about right now.

Chapter Sixteen

Ollie peered across the street from the sheriff's office, not surprised. Jonah, wearing a designer suit, the kind that used to make her drool every time she saw him, propped against the storefront of the laundromat. He tipped his head to her, like he was just hanging out, waiting for his spin cycle to finish. *What did I ever see in that guy? Broad shoulders, nice clothes, fancy date nights...* Yes, she had been that superficial. The truth hurt.

When he slipped a ring on her finger after only six months of dating—she, the junkman's daughter, felt so special. Why did it take attention from him to make her feel like she was someone? She swatted away the voice in her head, the one that wanted her to deal with a few things she had ignored for so long.

She glanced over her shoulder. Daddy and her brothers would be coming out of the sheriff's office in a few minutes. The doctor had said Daddy was fine, but he had made him promise to make a followup appointment as soon as he was out of jail. The last thing he needed was to see Jonah Blue watching them when he walked out.

She hurried across the quiet street as Jonah pushed up straight off the glass storefront. "What do you want?"

"What makes you think I want anything, Olivia?" Jonah smiled his bleached white perfect smile. "I might just be in the neighborhood."

"Yeah." Ollie snorted. "Did your maid break your washing machine?"

"The question is, why are you back in Red Creek?" Jonah reached over and touched the collar of Ollie's pink cotton shirt dress. "I thought you had finally taken my advice and moved on—for good."

Ollie slinked back from his hand and glanced across the street. "Look. Nothing's changed. I'm keeping my mouth shut. You don't have anything to worry about."

Rita Mayson stepped out of the laundromat door, a basket of wet clothes perched on her hip. "Well, as I live and breathe. Ollie Robinson, when did you get back to town?" Rita turned toward Jonah, and her eyes stretched wide. "Hello, Jonah."

Great. Now everyone and their dog would know she was back, which was inevitable. Soon, probably before lunch, Daddy, or at least one of her brothers, would know she had talked to Jonah. "I have to go." Ollie pushed a smile into place for half a second, then dropped it again. No need to bother. "Have a nice day, Rita."

"Oh, I will, honey." Rita's eyes sparkled, the idea of fresh gossip giving her a glow of pleasure. "Don't you worry."

Ollie hurried back across the street, not bothering to speak to Jonah. She looked over her shoulder once she was in front of the sheriff's office. Jonah and Rita disappeared around the corner of the laundromat, Jonah toting Rita's laundry basket and playing the part of the southern gentleman, the part he had down to a fine art. No doubt he was filling her head with fresh ideas of why Ollie had left town so suddenly.

"Alright, baby girl." Daddy, followed by Oscar, Oliver, and Owen, walked out into the morning summer sun. Ori was at work keeping the junk business up and running while Daddy did time, letting the other three brothers handle Ollie's business. Odi was at his law office. He didn't get involved in family affairs, but if Daddy didn't behave, they might have to drag him and his law degree into this one. "It's time for you and me to sit down and have a long talk."

Oliver was right. Daddy had lost weight. His tall, thin frame towered over her, the familiar dark blue eyes scrutinizing her as always. "We can, Daddy, but there's really nothing to tell."

"A pig's eye there's nothing to tell." Mr. Robinson patted the breast pocket of his tan denim button-down shirt, one of four that he had been wearing Monday through Friday for as long as Ollie could remember.

Daddy pulled out a butterscotch candy and started unwrapping the gold paper. Ollie lowered her gaze. Quinn did the same thing, popping candy in his mouth when he got agitated, trying to curb the longing for nicotine that never left completely. Did he miss her?

"Come on, Dad." Oscar, the oldest, the one that looked like Dad had spit out a carbon copy of himself, draped a muscular arm around his father. "Ride with me back to the house. We can talk there."

"House?" Mr. Robinson cut his eyes at his son. "I've been cooped up in that jail cell for way too long. I'm going to the store."

"Daddy." Ollie smiled up at her father, his scruffy jaw filled with grey and red whiskers from missing his morning shave. "Ori can run the store for a few more hours. Let's go home, and I'll fix a pan of biscuits and tomato gravy and fry up some pork chops. They're thawing in the sink." She reached up and touched his face with her pointer finger. "Besides, you don't want people to see you unshaved."

Mr. Robinson's eyes narrowed. "Don't think I'm slipping." His eyes traveled from his daughter to his sons. "I know you all are finagling me into going home. I'll let you this one time because I'm hungry and need a decent bath, but don't think you're going to start running my life." He turned his eyes back to Ollie. "And don't think you're going to get out of explaining things with food."

"No, sir." Tenderness filled Ollie's eyes. "I won't." She glanced across the street as her family disbursed to their different trucks. Jonah Blue was not going to hurt her father. She was back, and she'd keep her end of their deal, but the time for being bullied was over. It was one thing to take away her job and spread rumors about her and make her existence pretty miserable, but she would not let that man hurt her daddy. She'd chop off her right arm and use it to beat the snake into submission before that happened. It was time to man up.

After debating in his head about what to do for a couple of hours yesterday morning, Quinn had called Drake to tell him he wouldn't be in to work for a few days. Drake had not been happy when he didn't tell him why, but he'd get over it. If Quinn didn't have a job when he got back to town, then so be it. He had to get this right with Ollie. He'd thrown a few things in a duffle bag and headed out toward Nashville. Rambler would hang out with Poochie at Momma's while he was gone, so he didn't have to waste time trying to find a place for him.

The trip had gone slower than planned though, with an accident on the interstate from an overturned chicken truck bringing traffic to a two-hour standstill. That had been yesterday afternoon. He'd used the time to blow up Floyd's phone until he'd finally answered. Usually, the man was quick to respond to his texts, but not yesterday. Sitting in his truck with nothing to look at but the vehicle in front of him, he'd decided to just call the guy. "Hey, man. I've been trying to get in touch with you all morning."

"Sorry about that. I left my phone in my truck." Construction noises floated through the phone along with Floyd's voice. "What's going on?"

"Do you have the sausage dog guy's phone number? I need to ask Eric something."

"No, but I can get it for you." Floyd paused. "What's going on, Quinn? Eric wasn't around for a few days a while back, and everybody had to eat potted meat or whatever we could get from the gas station without his food truck open."

There was one thing you didn't do, tell Floyd a secret. He was great for getting information, but terrible at keeping it to himself. "I just need to ask him about something." The truck door in front of Quinn opened. He watched a man with a gut overlapping his jeans and stretching his t-shirt to its limit climb down and walk up the interstate to where a highway patrolman stood, sweating profusely in his grey and navy uniform. Quinn rolled down his window, and a wave of chicken manure and general chicken stench from having the birds packed together for the haul wafted up his nose. "Can you find out Eric's number and text it to me?" He coughed and rolled back up the window. "Hey, uh. Did the sausage girl ever turn up?"

"I haven't seen her at the food truck." Something loud banged through the phone in the background. "I got to run, man. I'll grab that number and text it to you as soon as I get a chance."

The number appeared on his phone later that evening as he pulled into a hotel in Memphis. Before he could go any further, he needed a plan... a plan that started by finding out Ollie's mother's name. He'd called Eric a couple of times but didn't get an answer. Probably because the man didn't recognize the number. He'd finally texted him before he climbed into bed. Eric, this is Quinn Lewis. Ollie left yesterday, going to Nashville to stay with her mother. Do you know her mother's name and address? I am in Memphis. I've got to talk to her.

He'd rolled and tumbled in the bed, checking his phone every thirty minutes until way past midnight. Now, today, sitting in his truck at the hole in the wall BBQ place where he'd eaten dinner last night, the humongous gaps in his plan, if you could even call it a plan, were blaring him in the face. Should he turn around and go home? How do you find a woman in an enormous city when all you have is her name? *I don't even have a picture of her.*

He took the last bite of the pulled pork sandwich and looked down at his phone as it rang. Drake and his momma had both called that morning, and he'd not answered either time. An unknown number with an Alabama area code appeared on the screen. Quinn snatched up the phone, almost dropping it with his greasy fingers. "Eric?"

"Quinn? Are you in Nashville?"

"No. I'm still in Memphis, but I'm planning on heading that way in a minute. Ollie left yesterday while I was at work." How much should he tell Eric? The man obviously cared for Ollie. He'd come hunting for her when she'd disappeared on him, just like Quinn was doing now. "She left a note—and I need to make things right between us."

"Her momma's name is Lucy, but Quinn, Ollie's not in Nashville."

"Where is she?"

"I heard through the grapevine this morning that she's back in town. Somebody saw her at the sheriff's office with her ex."

"The guy she left at the altar?"

"Yeah, Jonah Blue. I'm going to see if I can track her down after while when I'm done with the lunch crowd. Do you want me to have her call you?"

Her ex? Had they made up? Why else would she leave with him?

"Quinn? You still there?"

"Uh, yeah. I'm here." Quinn looked out through his windshield at the people walking in and out of the little storefront with their bags of food. Most were in groups of two or three, probably on their lunch breaks. Why was he here, chasing after a woman who didn't want to be chased? "No, that's okay, Eric."

"Look, man. I don't know what's going on with Ollie, but I do know that if she's with Jonah Blue, it's not because she is trying to get back with him. I don't know what went on between them to make her leave him at the altar, but I do know that she had no love lost where he was concerned."

Quinn barely heard what Eric was saying. She was gone. The memory of their kiss filled his mind, along with her laughing at him that day they were doing the dishes and she'd piled suds on his head, her bossing him about the kitchen; sitting beside him bawling her eyes out in church. "I've got to go, Eric." He hung up the phone and dropped it at his side. *I blew it, God.* He laid his head against the back of the truck seat and closed his eyes. *You brought her into my life, and I run her off.*

He lifted his head and started his engine. An old Willie Nelson song filled the truck cab. *The last thing I needed, the first thing this morning.* He snapped off the music and pulled onto the street. Time to go home.

Chapter Seventeen

"Hogwash." Orville Robinson stared across the table at his only daughter. "You snuck off without telling a soul where you were going. Don't tell me you were just out looking for a better job."

Ollie dipped the tomato gravy onto her plate and passed the bowl down to Oliver. "Dad, can't we drop it? I'm back, I'm fine." She reached to the center of the table and pulled a biscuit from the cast-iron skillet. "When's your doctor's appointment?"

"I haven't made it yet." Mr. Robinson pinched the corner of his biscuit off and dabbed it in the red gravy filling his plate. "Where'd you go? Oliver said you were staying in a nice trailer all by yourself. How'd you swing that?"

Ollie cut her eyes to her brother. He shrugged his shoulders and continued to eat, refusing to help her get out from under their father's interrogation. "I rode with a friend to Carson's Bayou, Louisiana. He stayed with his mother and let me stay in the trailer." She looked down at her plate. If Daddy saw her face, he would know she wasn't being completely honest. "I was looking for a job so I could find a place of my own."

"Uh-huh." Mr. Robinson drew his answer out, doubt dripping from his tone.

"What was Jonah Blue wanting?" Oscar, Ollie's oldest brother, sat at the far end of the ancient rectangular dining table. "I saw you two talking before we came out of the sheriff's office."

"Jonah Blue?" Mr. Robinson slammed his palms down on either side of his plate, rattling the tea glasses. "I knew it. I knew that man had something to do with your leaving." He glared across the table at Ollie. "Don't tell me you just bumped into him."

"No, sir." Ollie sent a death glare down the table toward Oscar. Why did he always have to try to be her second daddy? Couldn't he figure out he wasn't helping the situation?

"Well?" Mr. Robinson raised one eyebrow.

How did he do that? As a kid, Ollie had stood in front of the mirror trying to imitate the single eyebrow lift but could never make it happen. "He was waiting across the street at the laundromat when I stepped outside." Her jaw tightened as every pair of eyes stared at her. "He said he saw me and was wondering why I was back in town." She raised her jaw and met her father's gaze. "I'm tired of cowering, Daddy. I left him at the altar. I didn't commit murder or rob a bank. I'm not going to hang my head in this town anymore." *No matter what he's holding over my head.*

"You know how I feel about all this." Mr. Robinson stared back at his daughter, who looked so much like his wife. "You hold your head high. I never understood why you were skulking around like you'd done something wrong anyway." His eyes softened. "You act guilty, and people assume you are guilty. I don't know what went on between you two, but I'm sure you had your reasons for what you did. You aren't alone in this, Ollie. If you'd let me, I'd help you."

"We all would, sis." Ori, her happy-go-lucky brother, smiled softly from the other end of the table. "You say the word, and I promise you, Jonah Blue won't look in your direction, much less track you down like he did this morning."

The warmth of Oliver's hand on Ollie's shoulder helped strengthened her resolve. She looked around the table at her brothers, all there except Odi, who didn't hang around as much as everyone else. Ori had closed the store and came home for lunch, not wanting to miss the discussion sure to take place about Ollie's return. Her eyes finally settled on her father. "I know, Daddy, but let me deal with Jonah..." She looked around the table at her brothers. "If I can't handle him, I promise, y'all will be the first to know."

"We'd better be." Mr. Robinson leaned back in his chair and crossed his arms over his chest. "I know there's something you're not telling me about that man, Ollie. But you remember one thing. The Robinson clan has been in Red Creek for a long time. That rich ex-boyfriend of yours can't run any of us off, including you."

"Yes, sir." Ollie nodded. "I know that now."

Ollie looked down at her cell phone. She had dropped her phone plan a while back when she was working at the food truck, trying to save every penny for her great escape. This morning, she had paid the fee and restarted her service. She'd added Quinn's number to her contact list, not that she'd ever call him, but just knowing she could, made the hurt in her heart seem a little more bearable. Would he answer if she called? He didn't have her number. Would he recognize her voice and hang up?

She swallowed and blinked back the useless tears dampening her eyes. It would almost be worth getting hung up on to hear him say a single hello. He'd made it pretty clear; however, that he had wanted to keep his distance from her before she left. How he looked the day he'd gotten his hair cut pushed into her mind. It was the day she realized how handsome he was hiding under his unkept beard and shaggy hair. Even before that though, in the truck on the way to Carson's Bayou, how he'd treated her, a stowaway in his truck, how his deep voice had first said her name, how he smelled so good.... She rubbed her hand across her eyes. "Let it go, Ollie."

She looked at her cell phone again. She'd texted Jonah to meet her at the construction site this evening. It was time to set things straight. She listened to the crickets chirping in the dusk, occasionally drowned out by the traffic from the interstate not too far away. The hotel looked completed from where she sat near the temporary fence in Oliver's truck. The posh building cast a gigantic shadow across the deserted parking lot in the fading sun. Had she waited too long, been a coward too long? Did Jonah already have enough power to ruin both his and her father... and her town?

She'd stumbled onto the papers on his desk the morning before their wedding. He was skimming money from his father's business, lots of money. She'd wanted to believe that he had an explanation, that what she was seeing was a lie.

Ollie had gone to work for Gordon Blue as a file clerk after she'd dropped out of her second semester of college. The old man owned or was an investor in any business worth owning in Red Creek. He wasn't in politics, but if anything was going to get done in the town, Gordon Blue was the guy who made it happen. His funds made sure the school had state-of-the-art computer labs. His influence and money made sure the town's little hospital stayed afloat and staffed. Everyone loved and respected Gordon Blue, including her. Without Gordon Blue's money and support in Red Creek, the town would fall apart.

She'd started out as a file clerk, but after a year, Ollie had moved up and became one of the old man's three main secretaries. About this time, Jonah, Mr. Gordon's one and only son, had moved to town after living up north with his mother for the past two decades. The father welcomed the son with open arms and assigned Ollie to Jonah, who took an office next to Mr. Gordon.

Jonah swept her off her feet with his debonair style and handsome looks, taking her out of town to fancy restaurants and concerts and anywhere else he could think of to impress her. He'd bought her gifts, flowers, jewelry, treating her like a princess—all with money he was quietly embezzling from his father.

"Jonah." The day of the wedding, Ollie had crept away from the bridesmaids and met him in the choir room at the church. "Tell me you will stop." He'd looked so handsome in his jet black tuxedo. "If you stop and put the money back in your father's accounts, I'll forget everything. I promise."

"My father?" Jonah's lip had curled. The piano started playing the beginning of the wedding march. "Gordon Blue will never be my father. As soon as I get what is rightfully mine, we are leaving this town forever." He'd stepped over to where Ollie stood. She gawked at the man she was about to marry in a few minutes. "Forget what you saw, like you said. In two more years, Gordon Blue—my *father*—will be wondering why his company is falling apart while you and I will be living like royalty in Boston." He'd reached up and stroked the corner of her cheek. "I can give you everything, Ollie. Just forget what you saw."

"I can't, Jonah." Ollie stared. "Mr. Blue has been good to me, to the entire town. I can't be a part of this."

"Then you listen to me." He'd squeezed her arms, his face changing in a flash. "I can crush your daddy's little business. Don't think I can't. If you so much as breathe a word of what I'm doing to anyone—and I mean anyone—your father will lose his store, your brother Oliver will lose his coaching job at the school, Oscar won't be able to get an accounting job within a hundred miles. It seems like Ori has had a scrape with the law a time or two, so I'm sure I could dig up a little mud on him if I needed to."

Color drained from Ollie's face. "You wouldn't. Jonah, you said you loved me. You wouldn't do that."

"I would, Ollie. I love you, but I won't let you ruin my plan." He released her arms. "I can make life hard for your entire family. Do you understand me?"

Ollie ran out the back of the church, tripping over the designer gown Jonah had helped her pick out and paid for. Jonah was either half-crazy or just mean as the devil. He had played her like he was playing everyone else. He had lifted his mask for only a few minutes, but what she saw sent a shiver down her spine. She fled the church like Satan himself was chasing her.

Jonah had gone out and stood at the front of the church. He'd played the poor abandoned groom perfectly, just like he'd played the loving son and the wonderful boyfriend. Everyone had bought it hook, line, and sinker. Gordon Blue, of course, couldn't let the woman who had jilted his son continue to work for him. If Gordon Blue said you were a bad egg, nobody in Red Creek gave you the time of day.

"Have you come to your senses?"

Ollie's head jerked up from her phone, the sound of his voice pulling her from her memories like an icy finger running across her neck. She stared at Jonah. "I have, but not how you think." She looked at his perfectly combed blonde hair, his starched white shirt, charcoal gray dress pants, and shiny black shoes. Why hadn't she seen past all of this back then? "I'm staying in Red Creek. Jonah, if you so much as lift a finger against any of my family, I'm going to tell your father everything."

"He won't believe you."

"You're right, he probably won't." Ollie stared Jonah in the eye, refusing to look away. "But your father is smart. When I tell him to check on the hotel project, and the other accounts I saw that day, when I give him the details I remember seeing, he'll check into it." The corner of her lip pushed up into a secure smile. "All I have to do is plant a seed of doubt."

The arrogant look on Jonah's face melted away, and he tugged at his collar. "Ollie, listen. You are just as guilty as I am. You saw what I was doing and didn't say anything about it."

"I don't think your father will see it that way."

"What are you going to do?"

"I'm not sure yet." Ollie looked at the bully, suddenly devoid of his power. "I will let you know when I decide, but in the meantime—stay away from me and my family."

"This isn't over, Ollie."

She watched as his black Mercedes convertible pulled away, leaving her alone in the empty lot. The chain-link fence behind her separating the nearly finished hotel from the rest of the parking lot rattled as a stray cat squeezed through a hole and scurried away. What if Jonah called her bluff? The only name she remembered seeing on the documents was the hotel. Her head had been in such an uproar as she comprehended what Jonah was doing that she had quickly forgotten most of the details in the files. All she knew for sure was that Jonah was stealing from his father.

She walked over to Oliver's truck and climbed behind the wheel. Her hands shook as she started the engine. *Lord, I don't know where I got the strength to stand up to Jonah, but Lord, I'm scared. Please protect my family from him. He is not done with me, God. I know he is going to do something. Please don't let him hurt the ones I love.* Quinn's face flashed through her mind. Thank you, Lord, for having me leave him in Carson's Bayou where he's safe.

Chapter Eighteen

Quinn pulled his truck under the old oak tree in front of his trailer. The yard, the porch, the trailer all appeared to be exactly like he left it the day before, empty and lonely. He got out of his truck and fished his duffle bag from the backseat. The summer sun beat down on his head, but he was in no particular hurry to go inside where the air conditioner was sure to have everything cool. There was no need to wallow in self-pity. He slammed his truck door and started toward the steps. He'd done all this to himself. No amount of whimpering and whining would undo what his words had done.

He waved to Esther sitting on his momma's front porch across the dirt road. She stood and tugged down her blue jean shorts, then started walking in his direction. He had been dodging his mom's and Drake's phone calls ever since he left for Nashville. Neither one would understand why he dropped everything to run after Ollie, and both would probably give him an earful of fussing. His momma would because he had taken off chasing after a woman that she saw as a leach, and

Drake because he'd left the job his brother had helped him get when good jobs were not that easy to come by.

"Hey, stranger." Esther stepped up to Quinn and gave him a side hug. "We've all been a little worried about you."

"Yeah." Quinn shifted the duffle bag strap onto his other shoulder. "Sorry about that." His phone vibrated in his jeans pocket, but he ignored it. "I went to find Ollie." No need to hide from the truth. Everybody surely knew Ollie was gone by now. Momma didn't have a problem spreading his business to the rest of the family.

"I figured as much." Esther walked up the front steps beside Quinn and waited while he unlocked the front door. "Is she okay?"

"I think so." Quinn opened the front door and breathed in the icy cold air. His light bill would be through the roof this month, but right now he didn't care. He didn't care about much of anything at the moment. He dropped the bag on the floor by the front door. "Come on in and take a seat. I went to Nashville, or was on my way there to find her, but turns out she didn't go there." His eyes looked around the room, still clean from Ollie's efforts. "Have you seen Rambler?"

"He followed your mother and the kids to the pond to fish." Esther walked over to the love seat and sat down. "Do you want to tell me what's going on, Quinn?" Esther's voice softened. "You look awful. I'm a good listener."

"I drove her away." Quinn shrugged his shoulders. "I guess I figured she had nowhere to go and would be here when I decided." He shoved his fingers across the top of his scalp. "When I decided she was good enough for me." He crumpled onto the couch, his lips turning up in a sad smile. "Can you believe that? You know how I was back in the day. Me, with my wild past, still thought I was too good for Ollie." He shook his head. "I pushed her away, and she left. Now I just have to—get over her."

Esther stepped around the coffee table and sat down beside Quinn. "Look, I don't know what happened between you two, but I know you pretty well. You don't have a mean bone in your body. Whatever you said to her wasn't meant to hurt her. I'm sure of that."

"It really doesn't matter what I meant though, does it?" Quinn looked at Esther. "She's gone." He pulled in a deep breath and sat up straight. "I've just got to accept that." He patted his shirt pocket and pulled out a jolly rancher. "Right? I'll get over her, eventually."

"Like I got over Drake?" Esther raised an eyebrow. "If you love her, and I mean really, truly love her, you won't." She watched Quinn peel the wrapper off and put the candy in his mouth. "The hurt will be easier to bear on some days, harder on others, but, well, can I give you a little advice?"

"Sure." Quinn wadded up the candy paper and tossed it toward the coffee table. "I'm not doing too great with any of this on my own."

"Do you love Ollie?"

"Yeah." He rubbed his lips together and looked down at the floor where the paper landed. "I do. She's not what I was looking for. I mean." He looked over at Esther. "I wasn't even looking. Not really. Ollie sort of slammed into my life and took it over. But now, now I know that she's what I've been needing. It's like not knowing you need something until it's gone."

"Find her." Esther put her hand on Quinn's arm. "Don't let her get away, Quinn."

"She left, Esther." Quinn flopped back on the couch. "She left with some guy, probably her old boyfriend. She doesn't want me."

"Do you know that for sure?"

"It's pretty obvious?" Quinn rolled his head to the side and looked at Esther. "And why would she, after the way I treated her?" His phone vibrated again, and he slipped his hand into his pocket and pulled it out.

"Listen to me." Esther stood and frowned down at Quinn. "You can stay here and wallow around in your self-pity or go find Ollie and make things right." She put her hands on her hips. "I've never known you Lewis men to be whiners, but hey, what do I know?"

Quinn glanced down at the text from Eric.

> Ollie's brother Oliver picked her up from your place because her father was in jail. Here's her number. Do yourself a favor and call her.

He looked at the number and then up at Esther, his mind whirling. Her brother? Not her old boyfriend?

He stood from the couch and glanced around the room. "Where's my bag? There it is." He smiled at Esther, staring at him like he had a third eye on his forehead. "Can you tell Momma and Drake I'll call them tonight?"

"Where are you going?"

"Red Creek, Alabama." He stepped past Esther and paused, kissing her on the cheek. He picked up his bag and opened the front door. "And you're right. Lewis' men aren't whiners."

Ollie adjusted her behind on the hard, wooden stool and looked across the counter of her daddy's store. When she'd gotten the job as a file clerk for Gordon Blue, she'd swore she'd never step foot behind this counter again. She'd kept that promise until today, even when it meant working as a sausage slinger in a food truck. Now things were different.

She wasn't trying to protect her family by separating herself from them. If Jonah Blue dared to come after her by hurting her father or brothers, she'd stand up to him. Let the rest of Red Creek think she was slinking back home because she couldn't make it on her own. What did that matter anyway? As long as she had made it right with God and her family, let the rest of the world think what they wanted.

But you haven't made it right with God. That nagging voice, the one she'd been ignoring forever, whispered softly in her brain. *If you were right with God, you'd quit lying to everyone.*

She didn't lie to everyone. Ollie leaned forward and rested her elbows on the counter, propping her chin in her hands. She'd not told her daddy everything that was going on, or her brothers... or Quinn. She swallowed, pushing down the lump closing up her throat. If she'd been honest with Quinn, he would have thought she was a selfish coward. *You are a selfish coward.*

But what choice did she have? She was alone and doing the best she could. *You were not alone.* The whisper in her ear grew louder, refusing to be ignored. *God has always been with you, even when you push Him away. Even when you love yourself more than Him.*

She didn't do that. She didn't push God away. Ollie tilted her head down into her hands and massaged her eyes with her fingertips. She went to church every Sunday, even when she was in Carson's Bayou. She didn't let not knowing a soul in town keep her from going to church. Surely that meant she loved God. *Every time you lie, Ollie, you are choosing your way over God's way. You know that.*

"Honey?" Dad's voice broke through Ollie's thoughts. "You alright?"

Ollie lifted her head and looked up at Mr. Robinson. "Daddy, are you ever?" Ollie paused, looking for the right words. "Tempted? Like you know what the right thing to do is, but you talk yourself into doing something another way because it seems okay and it's easier."

"Of course. Just because we're Christians doesn't mean the devil doesn't quit trying to drag us into sin." Mr. Robinson laid a hand on his daughter's back. "In fact, I think the devil enjoys it more when one of God's children falls for his tricks than when a lost person does."

"What makes you say that?"

"I'm a father. When I see my kids hurting, I hurt too." He reached down and pushed a piece of hair out of Ollie's eyes. "I would do anything for you kids, even die for you. God's the same way, and the devil knows that. He can't hurt God directly, so he does it through God's children."

"But God forgives us when we do—stupid stuff."

"Of course He does, but if we love Him, really love Him like we claim we do, we won't listen to the devil when he tempts us. We'll trust God and do things His way, even if it is harder."

"What if we keep doing the same things over and over? Does that mean we don't love God?"

"It means at that moment, the moment we don't do things God's way, we make a decision to love ourselves more. We think, even if it's for an instant, that we know better than God about what is best. It hurts Him, but He's faithful even when we aren't."

Tears filled Ollie's eyes. How many times had she done this? Too many to count. "That's what I do. I know I need to be honest, but then I lie because it's easier—because I think my way is better than God's way."

"How has that worked out for you?" Mr. Robinson smiled softly at his daughter.

"Terrible, Daddy."

"Then it's about time you get serious with God—and

yourself. The Book says when you know right and don't do it, it's sin."

"Yes, sir." Ollie brushed a tear away with the back of her hand. "It's past time."

The bell over the front door jingled, and Mr. Robinson looked up. "Come on in and look around, young man. If you don't see what you're looking for, ask me. Chances are, I have it in here somewhere, or I can get it."

"Yes, sir." Quinn walked toward the counter. "You do."

Ollie turned to the familiar voice, her heart doing a somersault in her chest. "Quinn. You're here."

"I am."

"We need to talk."

"We do." Quinn reached the counter. "How about right now?"

Ollie sat up and wiped another tear from her cheek. She looked up at her father standing beside her. "Daddy, this is Quinn Lewis."

"Nice to meet you, sir," Quinn said, extending his hand across the counter to Mr. Robinson.

Mr. Robinson shook Quinn's hand. "You aren't from around here, son. How do you know my daughter?"

"Daddy." Ollie swallowed and sent up a silent prayer for strength. "This is the man I ran away with. I was living at his house in Louisiana while I was gone." Redness crept up Mr. Robinson's neck. "Daddy, remember what you said about God's way and all?"

"Yeah." Mr. Robinson's eyes glared across the counter at Quinn as he answered Ollie. "But, Ollie, you better start explaining a few things, or me and this boy are fixing to get up close and personal in a hurry."

Chapter Nineteen

"I don't know why you said your family is crazy." Quinn took a sip from his tea glass. "They seem pretty normal to me."

"You've known them all for what? Ten seconds?" Ollie rolled her eyes. "Hold that thought after you've been here a couple of days. At least Daddy didn't deck you or pull his shotgun on you. Besides, I said half crazy. There's a difference."

"I tell you what." Quinn grinned and propped his hip against the long counter in the narrow Robinson kitchen. "When you were telling him I was the man you rode off with, his grip went from a friendly shake to a vice clamp in about three seconds. It felt like he was going to break my fingers off."

"When his neck gets red, it's time to run for cover." Ollie stirred the enormous pot of field peas on the stove and turned down the burner. "But overall, I think he took everything pretty good." She turned and looked at Quinn, biting her lower lip. "The ham's baking, the peas are going, I'll get the corn bread stirred up. All that leaves is the mac and cheese. I'll be right back."

Quinn watched Ollie disappear out the door near the stove at the end of the narrow rectangular room. He didn't know a lot about kitchens, but this was the oddest shaped one he'd ever been in. It was more like a hallway with a sink on one end, a stove on the other, and cabinets running the length of the room on either side. You pretty much had to turn sideways to pass each other, and where was the refrigerator?

"Do you mind looking under there and getting that pot to boil the noodles in?" Ollie reappeared through the doorway, her arms loaded with a gallon of milk, butter, and two enormous blocks of cheese. "I'll stir this up and get it in the oven, then we can take a break."

"Don't forget the cornbread." Quinn squatted down in front of the cabinet Ollie pointed at and pulled out a huge boiler. "This one? How much macaroni are you planning on making?"

"Enough." Ollie plopped the cold ingredients down on the small counter space by the stove. "Yeah. That's it. Fill it about half-way with water."

Quinn did as he was told, then stepped across the room and put the pot on the stove. He breathed in the honeysuckle scent radiating from Ollie's nearness. She faced the counter, her back to him as she opened the ingredients and started working her magic with the food staples. "Ollie, I need to tell you something." He watched her body grow still with his words. "I never should have said what I said." His eyes drank in her blond hair stuck in some kind of knot on the back of her head, pieces hanging loosely onto her slender neck. What would the skin on her neck feel like under his fingers? "I want you in my life—now, not later."

"Will you, uh, step over there and get that cheese grater for me?" Ollie didn't turn around.

"Okay." Quinn stepped back, bumping into the cabinets behind him. "Where at?"

Ollie looked over her shoulder and nodded that it was further down. "The ones up top in the middle."

Quinn turned and opened a cabinet filled with little bowls, electric gadgets, and things he'd never seen before. "Is this it?" He pulled out a contraption and looked at Ollie.

"That's a juicer." Ollie turned and stepped across the narrow space. She reached up and pulled out a silver box looking thing covered in prickly holes. She pulled it down between them, holding it like a shield against her chest. "Haven't you ever grated cheese before?"

"No." Quinn's hands covered Ollie's over the contraption, and his heart did a flip. "There are a lot of things I've never done, especially in the kitchen."

Ollie's eyes stretched wide, twinkling with mischief. "Quinn Lewis, are you trying to make a play on me right here in my daddy's house?"

"No, ma'am." Quinn's voice, deep with a longing that had driven him, pushed him to find this woman, purred from his chest. "I'm not that kind of man." His fingers reached up and glided down her cheek. "I'm the kind of man that is finally seeing the woman he wants to spend the rest of his life with. The idiot of a man that almost let her get away because he couldn't see the forest for the trees." He leaned forward, his eyes searching Ollie's face as his lips found hers. The explosion of heat took him over as his arms wrapped around hers, the distant sound of the metal grater hitting the wooden floor barely registering in his brain.

"Well, well, well. Looks like there's some cooking going on in this kitchen, and I don't mean the peas."

Quinn felt Ollie pushing him away. He opened his eyes

and looked over at one of her brothers. His brain snapped back from where it had been going seconds before. *Which brother is that?* "Hey..."

"Ori." The brother leaned against the doorframe, grinning. "Don't let me stop you two."

"Shut up, Ori." Ollie squatted down and picked up the cheese grater. "We were just..."

"No need to explain to me, little sister, but if I'd been Pops or Oscar, well, that would have been a different story."

Quinn watched Ollie stand and step back over to the stove. "It wasn't what it..." He looked from Ollie to her brother. "I mean, it was, but I have plans."

Ori's grin broadened. "It's all good, Quinn. Ollie can take care of herself. If she thinks it's a good idea to be smooching with a man that Daddy just met a few hours ago right here in the kitchen, then hey, I'm all for it." He raised his arm, blocking the bag of macaroni noodles Ollie torpedoed toward his head. "Supper should be pretty interesting."

"Out." Ollie squatted again and retrieved the bag of macaroni from the floor. She looked from Ori to Quinn. "Everybody out so I can get this meal cooked."

"But." Quinn looked at Ollie, one hand on her hip, the other pointing toward the doorway filled with her brother. "We need to..."

"Not now." Ollie tilted her head to the side, her eyes stretching even wider. "I have to think, and you have to cool off."

Quinn stepped past Ollie, the honeysuckle scent sending another wave of longing through him. "Tonight?"

"Yeah." Ollie swallowed. "Tonight—but just talk, Quinn."

"That's all I meant to do, then."

"I like the way y'all have of talking." Ori's laughing words came from the hallway.

Quinn ducked as the yellow block of cheese flew past his head toward Ori. "Just talk. I promise."

The rest of his life. That had been his words. Ollie's forearms, covered with enormous red oven mitt's old and stained from years of use, reached into the oven and pulled out the iron skillet. She breathed in the aroma of freshly baked cornbread, and her stomach let out a low growl. Ori and Quinn had disappeared an hour ago after the... kiss. Ori said he was going to drive Quinn around town and take him to meet Odi, the one brother smart enough to not be neck deep in the latest Robinson drama. He'd met the others that afternoon after she'd explained to her daddy how she'd basically thrown herself into Quinn's life. She related how he'd been a perfect gentleman through the entire ordeal.

Daddy had listened, asked a lot of questions, especially about the sleeping arrangements, and then slapped Quinn on the back and invited him to supper. That was Daddy's way. If he liked you, he liked you. If he didn't, he didn't, simple. He'd taken Quinn to Oscar's office and introduced him. They'd left Ollie at the store to mind the counter. Apparently, the rest of the clan, minus Odi, had met Quinn while they were gone, too. That was good. They needed to get along.

Ollie frowned. Why had Daddy suggested Quinn drive her to the house so she could start dinner? Had Quinn told Daddy something about their relationship? She fumbled with the weighty skillet, nearly dumping the cornbread onto the floor. Quinn had followed her here. That had to mean he had feelings for her. Her heart soared with hope when he stepped into the store earlier. Hearing his words a while ago...

She pulled off the oven mitts and tossed them onto the

counter. His being here didn't change all the other mess going on in her life. Drama she had to deal with, had to clean up before—before what? She turned off the oven. Why couldn't the rest of her life be as easy, as enjoyable as cooking? Cooking came so easily. How come everything else came so hard?

She walked to the other end of the narrow kitchen and opened a cabinet door, pulling out a stack of mismatched plates. She couldn't start anything with Quinn until she straightened everything out with Jonah. What could she do about that? Jonah had everyone fooled into thinking he was Gordon Blue's perfect son, here to help dear old dad turn Red Creek into a nice little tourist town for visitors on their way to the Alabama beach scene.

The plates clanked against the old wooden table as she moved around the dining room, dropping each one in front of a chair. She would go to Mr. Gordon, like she had told Jonah she would. She had been bluffing, but the idea was the only thing she had. She had to do something. It was wrong to let Jonah get away with stealing from his father.

Mr. Gordon loved Jonah, his son he lost in an ugly divorce a long time ago. Would he do like she said and look into Jonah's handling of the company? If he didn't, what would happen? The old man believed she left his son at the altar, betrayed his son, as well as his trust. She dropped the last plate onto the table and rubbed her eyes. This wasn't going to be easy, but it had to happen.

She glanced over her shoulder at the noise coming from outside. Trucks pulled into the front yard, the doors slamming. Men's voices mixed with laughter floated into the dining room. Her heart squeezed, love rippling through her gut for every one of them... even Quinn... especially Quinn. How could fear and joy both share the same spot inside her heart? He loved her, too. That's what his words and actions meant. It had to be. *Lord, I need your help. I don't want to mess this up. I want to start new with Quinn. Give me courage to talk to Gordon Blue, to stand up to Jonah. Let Mr. Gordon see the truth, please, God. He has to.* She finished the silent plea and headed to the kitchen.

"Everything smells so good."

Ollie turned. Quinn stood in the kitchen doorway, always polite, always putting her first. "Quinn." She wiped her hands on the dish towel tucked into the waist of her jeans. "How long are you planning on staying in Red Creek?"

"I'm not sure." He stepped into the kitchen and took the pitcher of tea Ollie handed to him. "I didn't make a lot of plans on the way here." He smiled. "As a matter of fact, I'm not even sure where I'm gonna sleep tonight."

"You can sleep in the extra bed in Ori's room." Ollie slipped on the oven mitts and bit her lower lip. "Can we put off our talk until tomorrow night?" A puzzled hurt fell across Quinn's face, and her heart ached. "I want to talk about everything. I really do, but first I have to get some things straightened out."

"I can help you straighten out whatever it is, Ollie."

"Not this." Ollie lifted the pan of mac and cheese from the stovetop. His face looked so somber, doubt filling his eyes. "If you will hang around, if you'll give me time to get a few things settled, then we can talk." She swallowed. "Will you do that for me?"

"I'll do whatever it takes, Ollie. I meant what I said about spending the rest of my life with you. Right now, I don't have a job and my family thinks I've lost my mind. I don't know a lot of things, but I do know that you're the one, Ollie Robinson. I'm here and I'm not going anywhere until you force me to and that won't be easy. I'm not a great catch, but I'm going to do my best to be the man you deserve."

Chapter Twenty

Ollie glanced over at Oliver as he pulled into the parking lot of Gordon Blue's office complex. She had ridden into town with him after breakfast, leaving Quinn home with Daddy to do whatever. She had to focus on what needed to be done about Jonah. Quinn and Daddy would have to take care of each other for now.

Oliver hadn't asked questions when she said she needed to go to Gordon Blue's office. He had basketball practice with the high school boys at the gym. "If you need me, call me." He looked across the seat at Ollie, his brow wrinkled. "I'll come right back."

He would too. Oliver didn't fly off the handle like she and Daddy did. He didn't get in other people's business like Oscar and Ori either, or ignore things like Odi. He simply made himself available. "I'm just going to talk to Mr. Gordon. I'll be fine." Ollie climbed out of the truck and waited as the window rolled down. "I'll text you when I'm done. Don't worry."

"I can't make any promises." Oliver smiled. "You're the only twin I have."

"Same here." Ollie smiled back. "I'm also the tough twin."

Oliver laughed as the window rolled back up. Ollie pulled her shoulders back and watched his truck pull out of the lot. Time to live up to all the bravado. Bile rose in her throat, but she forced it down. This had to be done. Today. She stepped inside the office of Gordon Blue. The gooseflesh on her arms could have been because Gordon liked to keep the building cold enough to freeze ice, but it was probably because of the dread gnawing at her gut.

The offices opened at nine, but Sandra, Mr. Gordon's longtime office manager, never got there before nine-fifteen. Today was no exception. Ollie glanced around the empty office. Jonah's door on the right side of the building was closed. Good, maybe she could get in, talk to Mr. Gordon, and get out without anyone seeing her. She stepped over to the left of the room and tapped on the door.

"Come in."

Ollie opened the door and slipped inside. "Mr. Gordon." His gray-hair, wavy and combed to the side, hadn't changed a bit since the last time she had been in this office. That was before Jonah had come along, before all the junk he had caused. She stared at his face. They had been close before Jonah. He'd treated her almost like his own daughter.

"Ollie." Mr. Gordon's brow raised. After a few seconds, a gentle smile settled on his lips. "Come in and take a seat. I've been worried about you."

Ollie released her breath. She eased into the chair across the desk from where Mr. Gordon sat. Not getting thrown out on her ear was a good start. "I'm sorry I worried you. I had to..." The words trailed away, and she looked down at the small blue flower design on her dress. It was probably best not to start the conversation with how she had run away to escape the persecution stemming from his son's malicious gossip. She lifted her head and smiled. "You look well. I think you've lost some weight."

"I have." Mr. Gordon chuckled. "That new lady doctor has me on a diet, and I'm swimming a couple of laps in the pool every evening."

"Good for you." Ollie licked her lips, her mouth dry. "I'm glad you're taking care of yourself."

"I can see you've got something on your mind, Ollie. Before you tell me what it is, I want to say something."

"Okay." Ollie rubbed her palms together. *Stay calm, keep smiling*.

"I don't know everything that went on between you and Jonah, but I understand things have not been," he paused, his forehead wrinkling, "easy for you—since that day."

"No, sir."

"I'm sorry for my part in all that. I was upset when I let you go." The old man looked down at his desk and fiddled with a piece of paper. He turned his eyes back to Ollie. "I could have handled everything better. I've had my head stuck in the sand since then, but when you left town, I realized how rough all of this was for you, too."

"That's why I'm here." It was now or never. "I don't know what reason Jonah gave you for our, uh, break up." Her leg started to bounce, and she pushed it down with her palm. "The day before the wedding, I saw some papers Jonah had." She stared at Mr. Gordon's face, changing from compassion to curiosity. "Mr. Gordon, your son is robbing you blind. I'm not asking you to do anything but look into what you put him over—the new hotel by the interstate, the restaurant plans and movie theater plans. Just look into it."

"You." Mr. Gordon's eyes narrowed. "You know this? For sure?"

"Yes, sir." The door behind Ollie opened, and she turned.

"Dad." Jonah Blue smiled at his father, then looked at

Ollie, his smile never changing. "Ollie. Nice to see you. I heard you were back in town."

"Ollie." Mr. Gordon stood and walked around his desk. "I'm so glad you dropped in. If I get an opening for a clerk, I'll give you a call."

Ollie stood, her knees quaking. Did he believe her? He had to believe her. Why else would he be covering for her? "Thank you, Mr. Gordon."

Mr. Gordon patted Ollie's shoulder, then looked at Jonah. "Take a seat, son. I'll show Ollie out, then we can talk."

Ollie glanced at Jonah as Mr. Gordon guided her past him to the door. What would he do now? Nothing good. Her insides quivered as she lifted her chin. "Jonah. Have a good day."

"Oh, I always do, Ollie." He smiled like the shark he was. "I always do."

Quinn rubbed his hand across his jaw, stifling a yawn. He couldn't blame the lumpy mattress on the spare bed for his lack of sleep. He couldn't blame Ori's snoring from the other side of the room. He wouldn't have slept, no matter where he'd been. He'd seen Ollie for about five minutes before she left earlier that morning. The house only had one bathroom, and since he had no idea how they did things around the Robinson home, he'd waited until everyone else seemed to be done with their morning rituals before he went in. By the time he was done, Ollie and Oliver were walking out the door.

"More hotcakes, Quinn?" Mr. Robinson lifted three enormous pancakes onto his own plate from the platter between them. "The only family sit down meal we have around here during the week is supper. Everybody grabs breakfast and lunch when they can." He chuckled as he lifted the jar of cane syrup and drenched the pancakes. "I have to say, though, it's pretty nice having you here this morning. We haven't had hotcakes in a month of Sundays. With Ollie gone, corn flakes had become a staple."

Quinn looked at the last two pancakes on the platter. Ollie must have gotten up early to fry the enormous stack that had been there when he'd walked through earlier on his way to the bathroom. "I think I'll just take this slice of bacon." He picked up a strip fried to perfection. "Your daughter sure can cook."

"She takes after my sister, Sadie." Mr. Robinson picked up the last strip of bacon from the platter and looked across the table at Quinn. "Ollie's momma had a lot of good qualities, but cooking wasn't one of them."

Quinn took a bite from the bacon. Should he ask where Ollie had gone? Should he ask about Ollie's mother?

"Son, do you know the Lord? I'm not asking if you just go to church. Do you really know the Lord?"

"Uh." Quinn stopped the bacon halfway between his mouth and the plate. This man didn't beat around the bush when he wanted to find something out. "Yes, sir. I got saved not too long ago, as a matter of fact."

"Good. I can tell you have a soft spot for Ollie, and I like you." He poked the bacon in Quinn's direction like an orchestra leader's baton. "I made the mistake with Jonah Blue thinking that because he warmed a pew that he was a believer. I'm not doing that again."

"Sir." Quinn laid down his half-eaten bacon. "Can you tell me what happened between Ollie and Jonah Blue?"

"I can tell you what I know, which isn't much. We were at the church. I was waiting to walk her down the aisle, but she never showed up." Mr. Robinson bit off the end of his bacon and chewed. "I didn't handle any of that very well. Jonah told everyone to go home, that Ollie must have jilted him." He shook his head. "I should have spoken up, defended my girl that day, but I was caught off guard."

"Did she tell anybody what happened? Stand up for herself?"

"She never has. She said she had her reasons." Mr. Robinson picked up his coffee mug. "Jonah Blue has turned this entire town against my baby girl. Makes me sick." He sipped his coffee. "That's why I had my little talk with him. That man turned three shades of pale when I pointed my shotgun at his gut." He chuckled and set his mug down. "The thing wasn't loaded, but it still did the trick. I just wish I'd done it sooner." Mr. Robinson pushed back from the table and stood. "I'm heading into town to the store. You're welcome to ride along."

"No, sir." Quinn stood. "I have a few things I need to do today."

"Well, make yourself at home." He blotted his mouth with his paper napkin and dropped it on his plate. "Watch out for that rooster when you go to leave. Sometimes he gets frisky and tries to spur people. I don't get why Ollie likes the old bird so much."

Quinn waited for Mr. Robinson to walk out the front door. He gathered up their plates and took them to the sink, stacked high with everyone else's dishes. Would they expect Ollie to do all the cleaning when she got home? He pushed up his sleeves and turned on the water. It wouldn't take but a few minutes to get this done, and she'd be grateful.

Twenty minutes later, he wiped his hands on a dishtowel and headed to his truck. It was high time to meet Jonah Blue, but how could he do this without making Ollie furious?

Something was wrong in all of this, and only Ollie and Jonah Blue knew what it was... and Ollie wasn't talking.

He drove through town and out to the hotel construction site near the interstate. He pulled his truck along the side of the road and walked past the danger and no trespassing signs along the temporary fence around the area. From the interstate, the hotel looked finished. The parking area where the construction crew had left their vehicles when he was working there before was almost empty. The parking lot out front had been poured, but the inside still probably had a lot left to do. Either way, this project was almost done. He walked over to the food truck, parked where it had been when he'd started work in Red Creek months ago. "Eric?" Quinn stepped up to the window and watched as the man in the sleeveless shirt pulled the link sausage from the griddle and put it in the warmer.

"Hey, man." Eric turned. "You're a little early for lunch."

"I just finished breakfast. What're you still doing hanging around here? This place is about empty." He leaned against the window and looked over at the hotel.

"I have a contract with Gordon Blue." Eric wiped his hands on the dish towel laying on the counter. "He's paying me a weekly fee to stay here and feed the workers in addition to what I make in sales. There's still some people coming in from time to time working on the inside, so until they're done, I'm here. What are you up to?"

"I need you to tell me about Jonah Blue. How do I get in touch with him? What happened between him and Ollie? Why does everyone think he's such a nice guy when he treated Ollie like dirt?"

"Let's see. He's the only son of the wealthiest guy in Red Creek. Go to the Blue building in town, and you'll find his office. I'm not sure what happened between him and Ollie." Eric paused and squinted his eyes. "What was the last one?

Oh, yeah, the nice guy. His father, Gordon Blue, is sort of the pillar of the community and he really is an upstanding man. I think everyone has assumed his son is the same way. Jonah Blue comes off as a real winner if you don't look too closely. Know what I mean?"

"Yeah. I think I do." Quinn pushed off the side of the truck. "The Blue Building, huh?"

"That's where his office is. He drives a little black Mercedes. If you don't find him there, just look for the car. There's only one like it in Red Creek."

"I hope there's only one like Jonah Blue in Red Creek, too."

"You and me both, brother, you and me both."

Chapter Twenty-One

Ollie stepped out of the office building into the humid morning heat. She clenched her shaking hands. At least it was over. Gordon Blue had always been an honest man and obviously was a shrewd businessman. How would he handle his son's thievery?

She looked up and down the quiet morning street. She could call Oliver to come pick her up, but he didn't need to see her shook up like this. She pulled in a slow, calming breath, blew it out, and started walking. Once she'd walked out a little tension, she'd go to the store, check on Daddy, and call Quinn. She'd tell him about Jonah first. They had to make some plans. Was he going back to Carson's Bayou to work? Would he just come see her on the weekends? Was he moving here? Her lips turned up in a smile. Having Quinn nearby, no secrets between them, being a team, that would be.... The smile grew bigger. That would be amazing.

Ollie reached the end of the block and looked up and down the cross section. People were trickling in and out of The Whole Donut with little white bags in their hands. She pulled her phone from the pocket in her dress. Her hands weren't shaking, her nerves were under control. She'd call Quinn and get him to come pick her up.

"Hey, beautiful."

Ice filled Ollie's veins, and she turned toward the voice. Jonah sat in his shiny black convertible, his arm draped over the tan leather seat, smiling like he had the world by the tail. "Leave me alone, Jonah." Ollie shoved her phone in her pocket and started across the street. Jonah eased the car forward.

"Get in. We need to talk."

"Not on your life." Ollie clenched her jaw and looked around. Nobody seemed to notice them, but there were always eyes watching Jonah Blue. He loved being the center of attention, and the townsfolk loved accommodating him. "I have nothing to say to you."

"Daddy told me what you said." Jonah chuckled. "Nice try, Ollie." He eased the car a little closer to the sidewalk. "Get in. You'll want to hear what I have to say. I'm ready to get the Ollie Robinson noose out from around my neck."

Ollie stopped and glared at Jonah. Was he lying? She couldn't tell. Daddy could always tell when she was lying, even when others couldn't. He said her face told the truth even when her lips didn't. Jonah could lie to the preacher while taking communion and never bat an eye. "Tell me what you need to tell me."

"Not here." He nodded toward a passing car and smiled. "Do you really want to do this on the street? It's only going to get busier around here, and you know people love to talk."

Ollie cut her eyes up the street where Mr. Amos was unlocking his barber shop. The old man smiled and nodded in their direction before disappearing into the building. "Okay, but we can't go to your house. Your maid will flop her gums, and I won't stand for it, Jonah."

"Of course not." Jonah leaned across and opened the

passenger's door. "How about we drive out to the hotel site? We can tour the inside of the building. People saw you leaving Father's office. If anyone asks why we're there, I'll tell them Father hired you back, and I'm showing you the progress on the hotel."

Yep. He could come up with a lie at the drop of a hat. "Alright, but you might as well know that I'm not going to let you manipulate me anymore." She slid onto the cool leather seats and slammed the car door. "I'm done with being under your thumb."

Jonah pulled off the curb and looked over at Ollie, his smug smile sending icy shivers up her spine. "You really shouldn't feel that way toward me, Ollie. I've forgotten about our past. It's time for us to be friends."

"I'd rather be friends with a cobra. The chances of getting hurt by it are less than with you." She watched Red Creek disappear in the rear-view mirror. There would be people at the hotel sight, too, but they were construction workers, mostly from out of town. They wouldn't care what she was doing there, but they would be around to see what was going on in case Jonah decided to try anything funny. She glanced over at Jonah, his aviator shades now hiding his eyes. He couldn't hurt her. She wouldn't put it past him to threaten her, even hit her to try to keep her quiet, but she wouldn't get close enough. Not on her life.

Quinn pulled up in front of the Blue building and hurried inside. A woman, probably in her forties, sat at an enormous desk in the middle of the large room, looking at a computer screen. Black and white photos of different spots around Red Creek hung on the walls around the room. His boots echoed on the marble floor as he crossed the room, and the woman looked up.

"I'm looking for Jonah Blue."

"You just missed him." The woman smiled at Quinn. "He left a few minutes ago. Gordon Blue, his father, is in. Can he help you?"

"No." Quinn rubbed his hand along his jaw. "Do you have a business card or something with his number on it? Or do you know where he was going? I really need to talk to him."

"Hmm." The woman's eyes narrowed, and she opened a little drawer on her desk. "Here's his business card, but if you call that number, you get this phone, so that's no help." She looked up at Quinn and pressed her fingers to her lips. "I don't guess it's a secret. I heard him tell Mr. Blue that he had some business at the hotel site. You might want to look out there. Do you know where that's at? It's out near the interstate."

"I just left the hotel, and he wasn't there."

"Oh." The woman frowned. "Well, I'm sorry. I guess you'll have to check back later. If you'll give me your name and number, when he comes in, I'll have him call you." She quickly jotted down Quinn's information. She looked at the notepad, then up at Quinn. "You aren't from around here, are you?"

"No, ma'am. I'm in town visiting friends." Quinn looked around the room one more time. "Tell him it's urgent that I speak to him when he comes in." He hurried back to his truck. What now? Eric said Jonah's car would stand out like a sore thumb, and Red Creek wasn't that big. He started the truck and pulled onto the street. Might as well make a few loops through the little town and look for the black convertible. He looked at his phone. No text from Ollie. *Lord, watch out for her. I don't know what she's doing, but I know she will need you, no matter what it is.*

OLLIE LOOKED up at the hotel as they drove through the temporary gate and across the parking lot. A lot had changed here since she left Red Creek. The place looked completed. Where were all the workers? She turned her head, catching sight of the lonely food truck on the far side of the lot near the crew entrance. A finger of fear ran down her backbone. "I've changed my mind." She looked over at Jonah. "Take me back to town."

"This won't take but a second, Ollie." Jonah pulled around behind the hotel and parked next to a rear employee only entrance. "Let's go in. I want to show you the place."

"I don't care about seeing your hotel, Jonah." Ollie pulled the handle on her door. "If you won't take me back, I'll walk."

"No. You won't."

Something hard poked into Ollie's ribs, and she stopped. "What are you doing?" She looked down at the pistol pushing into her side, then up at Jonah. "Have you lost your mind?"

"Get out. We're going in the hotel, and you're going to tell me what you told the old man."

Color drained from Ollie's face. "I thought he told you."

"He said you wanted your old job back, and he was considering hiring you." He opened his car door and stood, keeping the little pistol pointed at Ollie. "I'm not the idiot you and he must believe me to be. I know you told him about the money. Now hurry up before I lose my patience and shoot you."

"Jonah, you aren't a killer. We both know that." Ollie opened her door, her hands shaking again. Why had she been so stupid?

"When your daddy shoved that shotgun in my gut, I realized something." Jonah waved Ollie toward the hotel door. "Anybody can kill if the motivation is strong enough." He stuck a key in the gray metal door, but it wasn't locked. He pushed it open. "You never should have come back, Ollie."

The hallway ahead of them was dimly lit. Ollie squinted as her eyes adjusted from being in the bright sun. She slipped her hand into her dress pocket and eased out her cell phone. She brought it down in front of her. If Jonah's eyes were adjusting too, maybe he wouldn't notice what was in her hand.

The pressure of the pistol reappeared on her lower back. "Walk. We're going upstairs." Jonah's hot breath blew against Ollie's neck. "It's a shame things turned out like this. I think we could have made a go of things if you'd minded your own business."

"If you think that, you don't know me at all." She curled the phone in her hand, hiding it from view. "I was blinded by your money and style and manners, but every snake eventually has to shed its skin. I would have figured you out."

"Don't you think you should be a little nicer to me?" The pistol jabbed into her flesh. "Considering the situation."

"You aren't going to shoot me." Ollie swallowed, her mouth as dry as desert sand. "People pointed the finger at you when I left last time. They'll catch you for sure if you do this."

They reached the end of the long, dimly lit hall and stepped through a short alcove into the front lobby. Sunlight poured through the glass front of the posh building. Ollie looked over at the dark wooden counter with the intricately carved molding. Her eyes traveled up, way up to the crystal chandelier above their heads, then across to the beautiful curved staircase on the opposite wall. An elevator was discreetly tucked under the curve of the staircase, and the entire room made Ollie feel like she had stepped back in time. A drop cloth with a skill saw and a few pieces of lumber were sitting near the front door, and everything needed a good cleaning, but the place would be opening very soon.

"It's nice, don't you think?" Jonah nudged Ollie forward. "I dropped a ton of the old man's money in this place." He chuckled. "He'll never recoup the money I dumped in this hotel."

Ollie's shoes clacked on the marble floor, moving to the center of the room. Should she make a run to the front door? Would it open? Would Jonah shoot her in the back? "What are we doing in here?"

"We're going up those stairs, and you are going to tell me exactly what you told Gordon." He shoved her toward the staircase, away from the glass doors and her escape. "I was planning on leaving at the end of the summer, just before this place opens and he realizes nobody in their right mind is going to stay in Red Creek, Alabama, no matter how fancy the hotel is."

Ollie's hand clutched the mahogany stair rail, ascending the steps upward. "You're intentionally trying to bankrupt your father? Why would you do that? He's been so good to you." Her eyes scanned the top of the staircase, fanning out onto the second floor. If she could distract him for a brief second when they got to the top, she could dart into one of the hotel rooms. If they were not locked, she could hide in there and call for help. If they were, he might shoot her in the heat of the moment.

"He hasn't given me anything that shouldn't have been mine all along, so don't even try that bleeding-heart routine on me. I'm taking what I want and leaving him to clean up the mess, just like he did when he left my mother years ago." Jonah put his hand on Ollie's shoulder, stopping her ascent three steps from the top. "This is far enough. Now, tell me exactly what the two of you said."

Beads of sweat popped out on Ollie's forehead. "Why are we stopping here?" She turned and looked at Jonah, smug, smiling. What was he planning?

"Because this is high enough." Jonah's lips stretched across his unbelievably white teeth. "A fall from here will kill you. I'll make sure of that." His face morphed into sadness. "She asked me to show her around, officer, since she was coming back to work for my father. I looked up and saw her falling, but I was too far away to help." He grinned again. "It's all going to work out even better than I planned." The grin vanished. "Now. What did you tell him? Don't make me get rough with you, Ollie. I'm not a violent man, but I will be if you force my hand."

"Someone will see you."

"No, they won't. Dear old Dad gave everyone the day off yesterday when we came over and looked around. That was nice of him, don't you think? It's just me and you, Ollie—just me and you."

Chapter Twenty-Two

Ford, Chevy, and Dodge trucks were everywhere, mixed in with the SUV's and cars of all makes and models... but Quinn hadn't seen a Mercedes anywhere. He drove past the high school again and started back toward the middle of town. What now? His phone vibrated on the dash, and he pulled onto the side of the road.

"Hey, man." Eric's voice floated from the phone. "I just saw Ollie in the car with Jonah Blue. Have you talked to her yet?"

"No. Where are they?"

"They're here. At the hotel. Jonah's car came in the entrance on the other side of the parking lot, but it was definitely him, and I'm almost positive that was Ollie too. The top of his convertible was down, so she was easy to spot. They went to the hotel. I'm sure of it."

"Thanks, Eric. I'm heading that way."

"I'll call you back if they leave before you get here."

Quinn ended the call and pulled onto the road, heading toward the hotel. Why was Ollie with Jonah Blue? From everything he'd learned, she definitely didn't have feelings for the man. It had to be about the thing she said she was going to clear up. Was she apologizing to the guy for leaving him at the altar? Should he wait, give her some time to make her peace with this guy? No. A burning nudge inside pushed him forward. He would check on her, make sure everything was okay. If it was, he would head back to Mr. Robinson's store and wait for her to make the next move. Something inside wanted him to check on her. *Lord, watch over her.* He pushed the gas pedal harder as he said the silent prayer, the feeling of urgency increasing.

A few minutes later, his truck flew through the gate and into the hotel parking lot. The other gate, the one Eric said the Mercedes had gone through earlier, was on the other side of the lot, closer to the hotel. He turned his vehicle in that direction. Why were they coming to the hotel? He sped past the food truck. No one seemed to be around, but since Eric hadn't called him back, he had to be in there or nearby. Otherwise, the place looked empty, no Mercedes in sight. He pulled up near the hotel's covered entrance and hurried to the front. The sliding glass doors in the middle were designed for the guests, but there were also swinging glass doors on either side of these for the overflow of people and the workers to use. They had often propped these open while working here, and hopefully they were still unlocked today.

He looked through the glass to the enormous lobby. The place looked empty, but a movement to the side caught his eye. He cupped his hands around his eyes and pressed his face to the glass. Ollie stood at the top of the staircase. Jonah Blue stood beside her with his back to the door. Quinn's heart started pounding at the expression on Ollie's face. Whatever was going on was not good.

He swung open the glass door, and Jonah and Ollie both looked in his direction. Adrenaline surged through Quinn's body as he took in the scene, the gun in Jonah's hand, the look of panic on Ollie's face. This man, this coward in his three-piece suit holding a gun against the woman Quinn loved, would not harm her. It would not happen. Not while Quinn had a breath in his body.

Quinn flew across the lobby, the clatter of his cowboy boots echoing through the cavernous room. He reached the bottom step and started up as Jonah turned. The shot fired from the gun, mixed with a shrill scream from Ollie's pale lips. The noises exploded in Quinn's head at about the same time as the searing pain ripped through his right shoulder. *That imbecile shot me.*

No, no, no! The disbelief pounded in Ollie's brain, refusing to accept what was playing out before her eyes. Jonah turned his back to Ollie, watching Quinn stagger backwards on the staircase. Quinn grabbed the rail with one hand to stop his fall while clutching his chest with the other.

Her arms reached out before her mind had time to process what she was doing. She shoved Jonah with everything she had left in her quaking body. Curse words flew from his lips as he catapulted head over heels down the staircase, landing in a heap, silent on the marble floor below.

Oh, dear Lord, I've killed him. A wave of nausea washed over her as the metallic taste of blood trickled from her lower lip. She quit biting down, releasing her quivering lip. Her legs weak and wobbly moved down the steps. *Lord, please don't let him be dead. I didn't mean to kill him.*

"Ollie?"

Quinn's voice broke through the fog of emotions swirling around her, and she stared where he sat on the third step, leaning against the rail, the front of his chest bright red. "You're bleeding." Everything that had been moving in slow motion, her brain, her emotions, her body, all regained their speed as she hurried down the steps and squatted at his side. "I'm so sorry, Quinn." The words mixed with sobs as she fumbled with her phone punching in 911. "You don't deserve all this mess I'm wrapped up in." She looked at his pale face, his lips almost white. "Please don't die on me. I promise to make everything right if you will just hang on, okay?"

"I'm not dying." Faint beads of sweat appeared on Quinn's forehead. "Hand me the phone. I'll talk to the 911 person." He nodded toward the bottom of the stairs. "Go check on him."

Ollie passed the phone to Quinn, too numb inside to do anything but follow his directions. Quinn was talking, making sense, so he had to be alright... didn't he? She stood back up and took a cautious step in Jonah's direction. Quinn's voice, telling the dispatcher to send an ambulance and the police, filled the silence. Would she go to jail for killing Jonah?

She could run again. Her knees quivered down another step. If she just kept walking, went out the way she came in, she could leave Red Creek and this mess of a life all behind. The nausea that had started at the top of the stairs returned, along with the conversation with her father. Running would be putting her own fears ahead of the well-being of everyone else... ahead of what she knew the Lord wanted her to do. Quinn's voice, explaining to the dispatcher how he had been shot, echoed in her heart like a convicting pound of a gavel. What kind of woman would run away, abandoning the very man who had put himself in harm's way to save her? Guilt washed over her like a freezing wave and she gulped, refusing to drown in the emotions.

She stepped off the bottom stair and looked down at Jonah. No, not this time. *Lord, make me brave. Give me your strength, Lord.* Bile rose in her throat again as her knees bent, lowering her down closer to the man who had manipulated her life for so long. She reached her hand out, hovering over his body. She needed to touch his neck or his chest, see if he had a heartbeat like they did on the TV, but her hand wouldn't cooperate.

She jerked her hand back as a low moan escaped his lips. She grabbed the nearby stair rail, stopping herself from tumbling backwards. "He's alive." Her voice sounded funny, too high-pitched. She eased back, away from Jonah to where Quinn waited.

"The ambulance is on its way." Quinn eased his body down onto the bottom step next to Ollie and wrapped his arm around her shoulders. "It's going to be okay."

Ollie looked at Quinn's shoulder, his shirt red with blood, his other hand pressing against the wound. "You're still bleeding. What can I do?" She looked up at his face, white as a ghost. "Quinn, lay back against the stairs."

"Yeah." Quinn leaned backwards. "That might be a good idea. I'm starting to see a few spots."

The distant sound of a siren filled the quiet as Quinn's head lolled against Ollie's, his eyes fluttering close. "Lord, please let me keep him a little while. I know where he's going if you call him home, but please, God, let me keep him with me a little while longer." She pulled in a ragged breath of air as her head stroked his damp forehead. "I need him, God."

"Oh, how sweet."

Ollie jerked her head up and stared at Jonah, staggering up, pointing his pistol toward her and Quinn. *Stupid.* Why in the world didn't she take his gun a minute ago while he was knocked out? "You'd better leave while you can." Ollie swallowed. "The police are coming."

"I know." Jonah straightened up, his face grimacing. "I may need a hostage to get out of here." He blinked his eyes, the gun shaking in his hand. "Get up, Ollie, or I shoot your boyfriend again."

"No." Quinn raised his head. "I'll go."

Ollie's head jerked back to Quinn, pushing against the staircase with his arm, trying to sit up. "Quinn." Her heart thumped like a bass drum as she slipped her arm from behind his head. She stood, putting her body between the gun and the man she loved. "Let's go, Jonah." She felt a tug away from the back of her shirt and glanced over her shoulder. Quinn had passed out again. "Now or never, Jonah. Come on."

"Here are my keys." Jonah dropped the ring of keys in Ollie's hand. "Get on the interstate and out of Red Creek before the police catch us and I'll let you live."

Ollie nodded, not daring to look back at Quinn in case Jonah changed his mind and decided to do him in before they left. "I can do that—if we hurry." She took the keys and held out her arm. "If we leave now."

"I know what you're doing." Jonah started walking, his gait more of a stagger as he headed toward the hallway he and Ollie had come through before. "I haven't forgotten about your friend, but you're right. I have to get out of..."

Quinn's body crashed into Jonah's back, cutting his sentence short as both men slammed into the marble floor. "Grab the gun, Ollie," Quinn yelled, wrestling against Jonah's body, pinned between him and the ground. "Grab the gun!"

Ollie reached down and pulled the pistol from Jonah's grip. She stood, holding the gun away from her body like it was a slimy snake. A movement at the front of the hotel drew her eyes. Eric barreled through like a tattooed linebacker and pulled up short, staring at the blood trail leading down the staircase, across the shiny gray and white marble floor, and ending with the two men struggling at Ollie's feet. "Help me, Eric! Jonah shot Quinn!"

"I think I have him." Quinn, even more pale than he had

been on the staircase, wobbled, his knee pinning Jonah to the floor, clutching Jonah's arms behind his back.

Eric ran over just as Quinn passed out again, tumbling over onto Ollie's feet.

"Here." Ollie passed Eric the gun as she melted to the ground beside Quinn. She glared at Jonah as Eric pulled him from the ground. "I can't believe I once thought I loved you."

"Touché, dear." Jonah laughed. "You deserve Red Creek. I may go to jail, but remember how they treated you here, Ollie. You've been in jail in this stinking little town for the last year. These people you grew up with turned on you and held you prisoner. You got away and were dumb enough to come back."

The lobby door opened, and two policemen rushed in. Eric shoved Jonah Blue toward the men. A few seconds later, two paramedics came in and started examining Quinn.

"Is he going to be okay?" Ollie asked, watching the paramedics load Quinn on a gurney. Quinn's eyes opened with the bumping and moving but drooped back close.

"I believe so, but we need to get him to the hospital." The paramedic counted to three, and both men lifted the gurney, allowing the metal legs to stretch out so they could push their patient to the ambulance. "You need to be checked over too, ma'am."

"I'll drive her to the ER." Eric wrapped his arm around Ollie's shoulders. "We'll be right behind you."

"I can't lose him, Eric." Tears rolled down Ollie's face as they walked to Eric's truck. "I've put him through so much, but he's stuck with me. I don't deserve him, but I can't let him go either."

"He's tough. I don't think a little thing like a bullet is going to keep him away from you."

Chapter Twenty-Three

Ollie paced up and down the gray speckled tiles of the waiting room floor in the emergency room. Mr. Robinson, Eric, and Oliver sat in the hard plastic chairs lining the walls, watching her moving methodically back and forth in front of them. The emergency room staff treated and released her over two hours ago. What was taking them so long with Quinn?

"Sit down, Ollie." Mr. Robinson's eyes tracked Ollie as she turned toward the double doors leading to the triage area. A nurse pushed an elderly man slumped in a wheelchair through the doors, and they closed automatically behind them. Ollie huffed and started pacing again. "They said they'd call you back when he was ready," he said, his forehead creasing. "You're going to be too worn out to see him if you don't sit down."

Ollie's shoulders slumped, and she walked over and fell into the chair between her father and her twin. "He must be bad off for it to be taking this long." She started to stand again, but Mr. Robinson laid a hand on her shoulder. A tear trickled down her cheek, and she leaned her head against his arm. "Daddy, if he dies, it will be my fault. I never should have gotten him involved in all my messiness."

"First of all, he's not going to die." Mr. Robinson tilted his only daughter's chin up and looked into her tear-streaked face. "The doctor told you he was stable thirty minutes ago." His big, calloused finger raked a strand of hair out of Ollie's eyes. "Second, he came here on his own. Didn't he? Didn't you say you had left him and he followed you here?"

"Yes, sir." Ollie swallowed, her throat thick with a longing to cry out her worries. "But he wouldn't have come if he hadn't..."

"Hadn't wanted to." Mr. Robinson fished in his pocket and pulled out a faded blue handkerchief. "It's as simple as that, honey. The man loves you. It's as plain as the nose on your face. Plus you love him too." Ollie opened her mouth, but he stopped her words with a raise of his eyebrows. "Don't start pretending like you don't. I can read you, remember?"

"Yes, sir."

"I'm not thrilled about how all of this got started. You should have come to me when you found out what Jonah Blue was up to." His voice softened. "I would have moved heaven and earth to keep you safe. I'm ashamed that you don't know that. You shouldn't have had to deal with that scoundrel's threats all by yourself."

"I do know that, Daddy." Ollie sat up and wiped her eyes with the handkerchief. "But the problem is, I would do the same thing for you." She sniffed. "That's what I was trying to do. That's why I didn't tell you—why I left the way I did." She searched her father's face. Her heart ached at the sadness in his eyes. "Dad, none of this is on you. It's all me."

"Quinn Lewis?" A man stepped through the double doors, interrupting their conversation, and looked in their direction.

"Here." Ollie sprang up and swatted at her tears one more time. "How is he? Can I see him?"

"He's still a little groggy, but he's going to be fine." The man put his hands into the pockets of his white coat. "Are you Ollie? He has been asking for you, even before he was completely awake."

"Yes." Ollie's head bobbed up and down. "I'm Ollie Robinson, his—friend. Can I see him?"

"Yes." The doctor looked at Ollie's tear-streaked face. "He's still getting a unit of blood and may nod off from the pain medicine he received, but you can see him. You have to promise me you won't fall apart or faint when I take you back. Weren't you the one that was with him when this happened?"

"Yes, but I'm fine." Ollie straightened her spine and pulled her shoulders back. "He got shot protecting me. I can handle whatever is going on with him, I promise. I just need to see him."

Ollie followed the doctor through the double doors back to one of many tiny glass-walled rooms in the triage area. The place was as cold as ice. Men and women in scrubs bustled back and forth from the many little rooms to a nurses' station in the center of the Arctic sanctum, chatting and talking to each other like all the craziness of the past few hours was a common occurrence here. As if pulling a bullet from a man's body was as common as taking out a kid's tonsils.

The doctor paused before opening Quinn's door. "He's going to be fine, but he will need to take it easy for a few days. We took the bullet from his shoulder without any trouble, but he lost a good bit of blood."

"Don't worry." Ollie swallowed. "He's going home with me, and I'm not letting him out of my sight."

The doctor smiled and pushed open the glass door. "Then he should recover just fine." Remember, don't get him upset. If you need anything, push his button or step out to the nurses' station and someone will help him.

Ollie stepped into the room, and the glass door closed softly behind her. She looked at the yellow curtain hanging from the runner on the ceiling surrounding Quinn's bed. *Lord, help me make him understand why I lied to him, why I didn't tell him about all of this. Lord, please put forgiveness in his heart.* Movement on the other side of the curtain interrupted her silent prayer.

"Hello?" Quinn's voice, weak sounding, but definitely his, filled the small space.

Ollie pulled the curtain open and looked down at Quinn laying in the bed. The blood-soaked shirt he had been wearing when they put him in the ambulance was gone. A thick white bandage covered his right shoulder and the corner of his chest. Different colored wires connected to sticky monitor pads on his torso led back to a box above his head. A thin green line floated across the screen on the box, showing every beat of his heart. Ollie's eyes traveled to the bag of blood and IV fluids hanging beside the bed. The color drained from her face. He could have died. The beeping of the heart monitor pulsed away in the silence. That bullet could have hit the other side of his chest, could have stopped the beating of his heart.

"Ollie."

Ollie blinked, pulling her eyes from the blood dripping rhythmically through the IV tubing. She looked down at Quinn's face, and his mouth turned up in a smile, his dimples showing like it was Christmas morning, and he had been a very good boy. "Are you hurting? I think your pain medicine has you a little loopy." She stepped closer. "Can I get you anything?"

Quinn winced as he scooted over on the bed. "Let that rail down and have a seat." He patted the bed with his hand, the IV tubing bouncing with his movements. "I've been telling them for the past hour to find you for me."

"I don't think I'm supposed to sit on your bed." Ollie bit her lower lip. The doctor had said to keep him calm. She probably didn't need to argue with him. "What if the nurse comes in?"

"What if she does? I just had a bullet dug out of my shoulder. If I want you to sit on the edge of the bed so we can talk, I think it will be okay."

"Okay, you're right." Ollie let the bedrail down and sat beside him, the warmth of his body sending a quiver through her. "I need to explain everything to you, but maybe I should wait until you get out of here."

"Before you start explaining, I need to tell you something."

Ollie's heart lurched. Was this it? Had she killed his love with her lies, her secrets? "I never meant for any of this to happen."

"You think?" Quinn grinned again and reached up, cupping her face with his hand. "I sort of figured you didn't plan on being held at gunpoint when you got out of bed this morning and whipped up all those pancakes."

Ollie leaned her cheek into his palm and closed her eyes, soaking in the caress of his hand against her skin. "You deserve better than me, Quinn." She turned her lips to his palm. "Ever since we met, all I've done..."

"Listen to me." Quinn's voice lost its playful tone, and his grin disappeared.

Ollie's eyes snapped open, and she looked at his face. This was it. He was going to break it off, politely, because it was his way, but he'd come to his senses. He was leaving her.

"I don't know everything that's gone on with you and Jonah Blue." His fingers tucked a stray blond hair behind her ear. "And I'll be the first to admit that you've led me around by the nose with all of your lies."

Ollie winced. Her gut tightened, bracing herself for what

he was going to say next. She would still take him home, still care for him until he was well... still love him... always love him.

"When I left Red Creek the first time, the time you hid away in my truck, I was lonely." Quinn looked at Ollie's frightened eyes. He dropped his hand from her face and picked up her hand. "I decided I wanted what my brother Drake had. I wanted to marry a good, God-fearing woman, settle down, have a few kids of my own. I had dated a lot of women, but none I'd ever want to spend the rest of my life with, certainly none I'd want to be the mother of my kids. Until then, I thought I didn't want any of that, but being away from my family for so long made me realize just how lonely I truly was."

He brought Ollie's hand to his face, putting her fingertips against his stubbly cheek. "When you came into my life, well, you didn't fit the bill for my ideal wife either, especially after I got saved." The corner of his lips pushed up in a lop-sided smile. "But Ollie Robinson, there is one thing I know for sure. It doesn't matter what you've done, I love you. It doesn't matter what you do now. I love you." He let go of her hand and reached up. He wiped away one of the tears running down her cheeks with his thumb. "If you leave me lying in this hospital bed and refuse to ever see me again, I will still love you. You stole my heart somewhere along the way, and if you leave me now, you'll be taking it with you."

Tears splattered down from Ollie's chin onto the sheet covering Quinn's middle. "I don't deserve you. I've lied to you from day one, bummed off of you since the day we met, only brought trouble into your life." She sniffed, and a hiccup escaped her lips. "I didn't mean to hurt you. I just didn't have the courage to tell you the truth. I took the easy way out and lied." A haggard breath heaved from her chest. "My daddy said that when I lie—when I sin like that —I am loving myself more than God. I have been so selfish."

Ollie's body fell forward, and she buried her head in his good shoulder. She lifted her head at his grunt and took a quick intake of air. "I'm sorry." She sat up, her eyes stretched wide. "Are you okay?"

"I'm fine." The grimace on Quinn's face smoothed out. "Here." He reached up and gently guided Ollie back down to his chest. "Your father is right, I think. When we sin, it's because we put what we want ahead of what God wants. We make ourselves our own gods. Being submissive to God doesn't come naturally, but God is faithful, Ollie. I think He brought you into my life at just the right time. He used you to bring me to Him. His plan for my life didn't line up with my plan for my life at first." Quinn stroked his fingers through her hair as his lips planted a gentle kiss on her head. "If you will take me as I am, I am yours. We can help each other be who we are supposed to be. All I know is I'm not me unless I have you."

Epilogue

THREE YEARS LATER

Quinn hung up the phone and looked at the spreadsheet on his computer. The profit margin was increasing at a steady rate and had been for over a year. He pushed back from his desk and walked out of the office and looked around the sparkling clean industrial kitchen. "Ollie?" He walked around the stainless steel countertops. Where had she disappeared to? The doctor said she could have that baby any day, but trying to get her to slow down and stay out of the restaurant had been hopeless.

"Can you help me with this?"

Quinn rolled his eyes and stepped into the walk-in freezer. "Don't you dare pick that up." He stepped over and lifted the box full of different meats she had picked out. "The doctor said to take it easy, remember?"

"I am taking it easy." Ollie leaned in, her enormous baby belly pressing into Quinn's side. "I'm just getting a few things together for Aunt Sadie. She's going to run the kitchen for me while I'm out with the baby, but I want to make sure she feels at home here before I have to be gone."

Quinn stepped out of the freezer and put the supplies on the counter. "Your aunt is more at home in this kitchen than any other person on the planet, except for you. She's been working here since the opening, so taking over isn't going to be..." His sentence faded away as he turned and looked at Ollie, a strange expression taking over her face. "What's wrong?"

"I either just wet my pants or my water broke. Where's the mop?"

Quinn looked down at the puddle at Ollie's feet. "Forget the mop. Get in the truck."

"We can't leave that on the floor. It's a health code violation."

"Woman, go to the truck. I'll mop up the floor."

Ollie looked down at the little girl laying against her chest. "She sure was in a rush to get here." Her fingers caressed the white fuzzy curls covering her daughter's head. Her tired eyes pulled up to Quinn standing beside her, looking ridiculous with his head covered in the blue hair covering. "I thought I was going to have her in the truck."

"Next time I tell you to get in the truck, maybe you will listen." Quinn leaned down and kissed Ollie's sweaty forehead. "What are we going to name her? Have you made up your mind yet?"

Ollie looked at the tiny bundle, her lips moving in a sucking motion, her face completely calm. "Maribel. Blessing and beauty."

"Maribel Olivia Lewis." Quinn smiled. "Welcome to the

family. I've got to go tell the Robinson bunch everyone is okay before they break in here to see for themselves."

Ollie's eyes drifted closed as Quinn walked out of the room. They had come a long way in a short time. The day Quinn left the hospital three years ago, the day Jonah shot him; he had insisted they stop by the justice of the peace and get married on their way to her house.

"We know this is right, we know it's going to happen," he had said. "So, unless you are wanting a big to-do wedding, let's go ahead and make it official."

She had not wanted a big to-do wedding, especially with all the gossip that started when people found out Jonah was going to jail for shooting Quinn—ex-fiancé trying to kill current fiancé. Tongues were sure to wag.

While the town had been distracted with Jonah Blue's trial and Gordon Blue's report that his son had been stealing from him all along, Quinn had healed up and quietly set about the business of making Ollie's dreams come true. He'd taken his life savings and put every penny into buying an old warehouse on the edge of town near the interstate and not too far from the new hotel. For the next year, they lived with her family and worked on transforming the old place into the restaurant with her name on the door. When they opened a year later, Quinn had taken over the business end of the place, including managing everything out front, so Ollie could do what she loved, cook.

They had moved into the second floor above the restaurant, converting it into an apartment. Despite Jonah Blue's predictions of failure for the hotel, the town of Red Creek was seeing increased traffic, especially during the summer months, and the hotel was flourishing. All those tourists seemed to love Ollie's restaurant and word was spreading that it was the place to visit while driving through their end of Alabama.

How had she, the liar and thief and runaway, ever ended up so blessed? Only through God's wonderful grace and mercy. The baby squirmed on her chest, and she readjusted her, waiting until the child was comfortable before her thoughts drifted into sleep. *Thank you, Lord, for your faithfulness to me, your undeserving child.*

IF YOU ENJOYED THIS BOOK, please take a few minutes to leave a review now. Authors, myself included, really appreciate this, and it helps draw more readers to books they may enjoy as well. Writing just a quick three or four words in a review makes a world of difference to an author. Thanks! KC

Look for book one in the Red Creek Redemption Series coming soon. In the meantime, check out all my other titles listed on the Books By KC Hart section.

I Couldn't Do It Without You

Thank you once again to my supportive husband, Mr. Wonderful, who encourages me to continue forward. Who lets me bounce ideas off of him and fixes problems like, what's a good hard candy to keep in your pocket besides peppermint or butterscotch? Duh... jolly ranchers.

Thank you to my oldest daughter, who always helps find the right blurb words, who asks how the writing is going and really listens to my response. Thank you for helping me come up with twists and turns to keep my story going.

Thank you to my ARC/Beta team. You ladies are so supportive and kind. You have no idea how much I rely on you in those weeks before the launch. You help me know I'm not in this ministry alone.

Thank you, Lord, for directing my path as I write these stories. I'm a lot like Ollie. I sometimes want to just run away when things get hard, but You, oh Lord, are always faithful. Thank you for giving me ideas, holding me up when I'm too tired to write, giving me courage to write my words down.

Blessing,

KC Hart

A Little About KC

KC sincerely believes that well-written Christian fiction can change lives. When a novel has strong Christian principals woven intricately into a well-written plot, the reader bonds with lifelike characters who struggle with trials, temptations, and struggles that the reader identifies with. The reader identifies with these characters because she's been there. Everyone has fallen. That's why everyone needs a Savior.

Then, when these same characters turn to Christ the Savior to bring them through these dark moments, the reader finds hope. KC believes the story reminds the reader why she must lean on the Lord in her trying situations. Through the book's structure showing Christianity as the positive light for good that KC knows to be true, the reader also sees why she needs to be the hands and feet of Christ to others.

KC strives to show how the Lord uses situations, people, and His Word to bring the lost to Him, and mold, prune and grow His children. She tackles challenging situations, powerful emotions, and spiritual warfare through engaging stories and true-to-life characters.

KC's favorite Bible verses are Philippians 2:5-8. Have this mind among yourselves, which is yours in Christ Jesus, who, though he was in the form of God, did not count equality with God a thing to be grasped, but made himself nothing, taking the form of a servant, being born in the likeness of men. And being found in human form, he humbled himself by becoming obedient to the point of death, even death on a cross.

KC cannot read these words without getting a lump in her throat. She strives daily to use her writing, her platform, her small influence to show others the love Christ has shown her.

If you enjoyed this book, please take a few minutes to leave a review now. Authors, myself included, really appreciate this, and it helps draw more readers to books they may enjoy as well. A few words are appreciated...
Thanks! KC

Join KC's newsletter and receive a free ebook of Music Smarts and Humble Hearts

Follow KC on her social media platforms

https://www.goodreads.com/author/show/20570083.
K_C_Hart

https://www.bookbub.com/profile/kc-hart?list=author_books

https://www.facebook.com/KCWRITESBOOKS

Books By KC Hart

A Christmas Blaze

Fresh Starts and Small Town Hearts

Business Smarts and Reckless Hearts

Car Smarts and Bashful Hearts

People Smarts and Wounded Hearts

Kid Smarts and Wistful Hearts

Family Smarts and Runaway Hearts

Elsie: Prairie Roses Collection

Moonlight, Murder and Small Town Secrets

Music, Murder and Small Town Romance

Memories. Murder and Small Town Money

Merry Murder and Small Town Santas

Medicine Murder and Small Town Scandal

Marriage, Murder & Small Town Schemes

Mistaken Murder & Small Town Status

Mistletoe, Murder & Small Town Scoundrels

Join KC's newsletter and receive a free ebook of Music Smarts and
Humble Hearts

www.ingramcontent.com/pod-product-compliance
Lightning Source LLC
Chambersburg PA
CBHW020332260626
47156CB00004B/1490